The Hill of Gypsies

The Hill of Gypsies
and other stories

Said al-Kafrawi

Translated by
Denys Johnson-Davies

The American University in Cairo Press

Dar el Kutub No. 2392/98
ISBN 977 424 480 X

Printed in Egypt

Contents

Translator's Introduction

Said al-Kafrawi is one of a half-dozen Egyptian writers practicing the art of the short story with distinction. Both in subject matter and in the rich language he employs, often drawing on a vocabulary that is in use among the peasants he writes about, al-Kafrawi remains uncompromisingly 'local.' If, despite his seven volumes of short stories and his reputation in the Arab world, he has not achieved recognition abroad, this is in part due to the fact that so far he has confined himself to the short story. Another reason is no doubt the singular difficulty he presents to the translator and, thus, to the foreign reader.

Almost without exception his stories have for their background the Egyptian countryside into which he was born. Though he now works in Cairo as a journalist, his attachment to his village—an hour's drive from the capital—remains strong and he pays frequent visits to the few acres of land he bought with his savings from several years working in Saudi Arabia as an accountant.

In his stories he is concerned, to a greater extent than others who have written of village life, with providing the reader with a feeling for the fabric of lives spent in the daily toil of gaining a livelihood from the soil and from the animals that intimately share the farmers' work and even their simple homes. He is also one of the few writers in whose stories we find animals playing a real role and not merely appearing as part of the landscape. Many of these stories are seen through the eyes of a boy protoganist named Abdul Mawla; perhaps it needs a child to be able to see an animal as more than an object that is translatable into that commodity—money—with which the peasant farmer is inevitably concerned. In "The Wolf Cub" we see the boy fascinated at acquiring a wolf puppy and his delight at the prospect of taming it. Against the advice of others, and his own fear of it, he is determined to have it as a pet. His father, echoing Islam's teachings about man's responsibilities toward animals, tries to persuade his son to release the wolf into its natural surroundings.

The child in "The Camel, Abdul Mawla, the Camel" lives in terror of these fearsome but tamable animals that are a part of village life. His family are ashamed of this unnatural fear shown by their young son and relate it to someone having put the evil eye on him. It is only when the evil eye has been removed that the boy finds the courage to overcome his fear. "The Boy on the Bridge" tells of the strange bird that has entered the boy's life and dreams, of his desire to touch and handle the bird, and of his concern for its safety from the hands of the foreign hunter. In "The Gazelle Hunter," the man who has mercilessly hunted these animals throughout his life comes to have a very special affection for them.

In stories such as "The Blind Sheikh," "The Night Book," and "Absence," the reader is made aware of the importance played by religion in the daily lives of al-Kafrawi's characters: the five-times-daily call to prayer from the local mosque, the Koranic school at which the village children start their education; the tomb of the local holy man, often believed to be possessed of special powers; and the simple belief that their lives and the times of their death are controlled by the Hand of the Almighty.

The title story takes place in the special month of Ramadan, a month of fasting with spiritual significance. The gypsy woman Galila, who passes through the village and tells the women their fortunes, is held in awe coupled with suspicion; she represents for them another world, a world of freedom, a world both desirable and dangerous. At the end of the story, the boy, in a kind of trance, has his heart cut out from his body by the chief of the gypsies and then replaced. In this apparently miraculous ceremony, the boy is recollecting the story about the Prophet Muhammad when, as a child, he was approached by two men who perform on him just such an act of cleansing with his heart.

The critic Dr Ferial Ghazoul has described al-Kafrawi's stories as being Egyptian examples of magic realism in which dreams, superstitions, and legenads are woven into the fabric of everyday life; through such magic realism the writer is able to give to his stories an extra dimension over and above the drama of daily events.

Villagers, basic in their wants and ambitions, are nevertheless deeply conscious of such abstractions as integrity and honor. They live in an enclosed world and once their daily needs are satisfied it is such abstractions that are important for them: the good opinion of their neighbor and the satisfaction that they have lived in accordance with certain teachings. Thus the story "A Matter of Honor" relates to the age-old problem, especially acute in the countryside, of a girl's honor and the shame that is borne by the family in the event of her losing it. In practice, such shame is often effectively wiped out by the immolation of the girl at the hands of one of the male members of her family. In al-Kafrawi's story the matter is resolved by the old grandmother of this aristocratic family with a cold harshness that she alone is capable of conjuring up. The starkness of its ending, like that of "The Man with the Traps" and others, shows the distinctive touch that this writer brings to the Egyptian short story.

The Hill of Gypsies

The Boss

Long ago, when I was a child—perhaps I was six or seven years old at the time—I would catch a glimpse of him standing at the waterfall that plunged down from the river to the small canal.

Behind him I would see the sun and hear the wind striking against the spit of land, and I would see the double-barreled gun slung across his shoulder. He would be wearing a red woolen overcoat, with a felt cap of camel hair on his head, and he had mustaches which, as they say, a falcon could have stood on.

"Uncle Shishtawi al-Addasi, be careful not to go near him—he's the boss of a gang of criminals," they would say.

With my father holding me by the hand, we were passing by where he was standing, and I heard him say, "That your son, Salama?"

"We're at your service."

"Let him come to me."

I was restive as a young donkey. I hid myself in my father's embrace, while he prodded me in the back with his fist—"Get a move on, son"—and I fought against wetting myself. When I got to him he lifted me up and I was trembling with fright and humiliation, sobbing in the face of the sun and the wind that carried his echoing laughter.

While sunbathing by the river like puppies after we had swum in the forenoon, we would talk about the young girls he had kidnapped, the grand houses he had robbed, and the lives he had cut short.

When I went to bed at night beside my grandmother, Hanem, in the second-floor room, with sleep eluding me, I would hear the neighing of his horse and its galloping hooves coming from deep within the night.

After that he was absent for many long years. When I asked my father about this, he answered me, "They put him away."

"How?" I asked.

"That's to say in prison," he said.

Throughout the years of my childhood and youth, whenever I passed by his lair on the river, I would look to where he used to stand, or to where he would sit in the midst of his men, his terrifying laughter ringing out.

Many years passed. Stories about him would shine like the blade of a knife and I would feel a longing for his fascinating presence and the days when he was out and about. I would ask myself, "Did there really live among us in this mud village such a man?"

Years are recorded by a sundial and, with time, the heads of men become tinged with gray. After some years I returned, having parted company with that young boy who used to have to hold his urine and at night would be frightened of the neighing of the horse and its galloping hooves.

In the place at the waterfall is a trellis of climbing flowers, a lemon tree, a date palm which never gives fruit, a eucalyptus tree, and a mud wall where puppies crowd around the teats of their dozing mother.

An old man lives out the final stretch of his life with bent back, blind or all but, beside him a water jug, while on a branch of the lemon tree a bundle of bread hangs, and there's a pit for a fire that has gone out and on top of it a blackened tin for making tea.

It's as though I know him.

The memory shines for an instant and lights up what oblivion has covered over.

"Uncle Shishtawi?" I whispered. It is he—there is no denying what one sees.

"Boy," I heard him calling.

"Yes."

"Come, boy, and take me home."

As I advance toward him, I feel, to my astonishment, my old fear of him still lurking inside me, though he is now a decrepit old man with bowed back.

I keep silent and utter not a word. With my hand encircling his waist, and with his arm on my shoulder, we start off.

I breathe in the smell of old bones and I realize that the man is fading away before my very eyes in his search for death.

We proceed toward his house, making our way along a mud track.

Absence

They brought me back from the other side of the river.

I had picked a quarrel with the children and had told them I would swim across the river, but when I had done so I was afraid to come back. I stood naked on the other bank in the noonday sun, filling the world with my wailing until one of the men swam out and brought me back. Then he handed me over to my father, who screamed at me, "By the Lord, you son of a bitch, I'll tan your backside."

I remember that day. I was standing naked near the oven for baking bread with the scorching heat striking against my body and my father beating me with a thin cane, while all the time my mother, with head bared, went on kneading the dough for the midday baking. She shouted at my father, "Instead of beating him, why not put him in Sheikh Ali's Koranic school, where he can learn something useful."

In the morning my grandmother Hanem dragged me along by the hand and delivered me to the venerable sheikh so that I might learn something and commit to memory God's Holy Book.

When she left me and went off, I felt that I was a stranger far from home and that I would not be returning to it. Suddenly I missed my mother and made up my mind to run away. But when I gave some thought to the school, which lay on the outskirts of the village and which had a view of the old mosque, I wavered.

In front of the school was a well with spring water and a mulberry tree close by that cast its shadow over the place. From the well the animals quenched their thirst, and it had an iron hand pump by which passers-by were provided with water, as well as those going to and coming from the fields.

The area of the school was roofed over with branches, and it had a dirt floor. In its courtyard was a guava tree, three green castor-oil plants, and a large jar made of porous clay from which the children would drink.

The children at the school were rounds of unripe flesh with shaven heads, in the center of which were luminous, friendly eyes.

As I stood hesitantly by the door, the boys stared at me and one of them called out, "Come in, boy."

On their laps were copies of the Koran, and I looked at them as they recited.

I walked through the door and the sheikh shouted at me, "Beside the wall, and sit down, you little devil."

I slunk down beside the wall and looked at the rectangle of sunlight that was penetrating from the door at this noon hour, and it made me conscious of the gravity of my imprisonment in this small space.

The reciting stirred my heart as I became aware of the intoning voices that carried the sacred words

to my hearing. I had the same sensation as when my
uncle would hold recitals of the Koran by blind
sheikhs in our house for the soul of someone who
had died.

I took note of her when I saw her sitting over
there in the corner—a girl amid all the boys.

I knew that she was blind from the way she held
her head slightly bent, and when she raised it I did
not find in her face eyes like ours.

Her face was as white as fresh milk. Suddenly my
heart was stirred and I felt peace of mind, an
affection for the place also. She was wearing a white
headcloth and there was a faint smile on her lips. As
I contemplated her small nose that was like a jujube
fruit, I asked myself: whose daughter could she be?

When I asked my neighbor about her, he
answered me, "That's Sheikha Aneesa."

"Sheikha?"

"Of course, man, she learnt the Koran by heart
by the time she was seven years old."

The sheikh ordered the boys to keep quiet and
asked Aneesa to recite.

Being but a beginner in the search for
knowledge, I felt something battering at my heart,
as though a door were opening before me through
which I could enter and find myself commanding a
view of the loggia of the mosque of Sidi Abu
Hussein, and I would see the poor sitting in the
loggia, from whose ceiling there hung a lamp that
opened the way for a gentle, compliant light that
looked down upon the place. I saw myself as
someone entering, then and there, as from the first

moment, a door which would give me an experience of wonder and by which I would come to learn the first letters.

From the very first moment I saw her I loved Aneesa, and our master gave me the task of bringing Aneesa from her home and taking her back each day.

She used to place her hand on my arm, and as I led her along the way she would talk to me, using strange expressions and opening my eyes to magic, to the six closed doors and to the final seventh door which alone contained the secret. I would gaze long at her, under her white head-covering, as I walked along with her as in a dream.

I was frightened that I would lose Aneesa and that she would go out of my life.

And indeed, Aneesa became ill and was absent from the school. I was to learn what loss and bereavement meant, and to have the experience of being consumed by grief.

I would go around from lane to lane, from alleyway to alleyway, aimlessly like someone in a fever, asking her mother about her until I went in to where she was. I placed my hand on her forehead and felt the heat of it burning my heart.

Aneesa made her final journey on a Friday. At that moment I felt I was an orphan and experienced my first sorrows. Depressed by the village, I realized that I was on my own after her sudden departure.

I became preoccupied with the idea of where people went after death. When I asked my old grandmother, who was sitting on a heap of earth, she replied that they go to meet the face of a beneficent Person. Then she added, "Death is the fate of every living thing, and life, O son of my son, ends with death."

Our master gathered together the children of the school, and we walked in front of the funeral procession, reciting in a sad tone verses from the Holy Book, carrying in our hands open copies of the Koran under the eye of the sun, which was scorchingly hot, walking along the dirt track traversing the fields that led to the cemetery.

It was my first visit to the graves. I saw that they were like kneeling camels, with the children of the poor riding on them in expectation of charity given for the souls of the departed.

I breathed in the odor of the earth and saw, through the opening of the grave, bones stacked to one side, and I held out against my tears. When I saw them carrying the girl in her shroud, I felt my heart split. I began wailing out loud, and one of the men took me in his arms to comfort me.

The Hill of Gypsies

My grandfather was at the threshold of the house, while I was stretched out on my stomach along the sloping date palm, astride it as on a bride. I raised my head and called out, "Grandpa."

Enveloped in a blue broadcloth cloak, he was peering in my direction with feeble eyes. I told myself, "He's back from market." Under the trellis the animals were chewing the cud dreamily, and the dog Antar was playfully running from wall to wall with the young billy goat. From before sunset cool breezes had been blowing, and the café radio had been blaring out in Ramadan the glorification of the early conquests of Islam.

"Grandpa."

He propped himself against the trunk of the sloping date palm, and I came down so as to be near him. "Did you water the animals?" he shouted.

"Yes, Grandpa."

"You mixed the fodder with beans?"

"Yes, Grandpa."

"Sprinkle some water in front of the house, then water the two orange trees and the olive tree, and let the young calf loose."

"All right, Grandpa."

Stretching out his hand, he brushed away the hair from my forehead.

"How old is the date palm, Grandpa?"

"Very old, as old as your forefathers."

"And you, how old are you, Grandpa?"

"Very old."

"From the days of Orabi, for instance?"

"And who's told you about Orabi?"

"We have him in our history book."

He smiled and patted me on the back. "Good for you."

There were some stones lying about below the wall, and the light of dusk was emptying itself into the sky before the sunset prayer of Ramadan. I looked into his face and remembered that whenever my father scolded me harshly for neglecting my studies, I would run to my grandfather and take refuge in his embrace. I would hear him telling my father off: "You'll go on at him till you do for him."

He used to seat himself, then take my head and put it on his lap, and I would hear him reviling unknown persons. I'd see him point toward the shade traced on the wall, while with his leg he would rock me to sleep and would not wake me until I had woken up of my own accord.

Plunging his hand into his cloak, he brought it out and waved it in front of me.

I was astonished when I saw the colored sun glowing behind him. Clapping my hands together, I called out, "Hey! A Ramadan lantern! A Ramadan lantern!"

I jumped to my feet. Whenever I stretched out my hand to take it, my grandfather raised it higher.

"God keep you, Grandpa—let me have the lantern, don't tease me."

He burst out laughing and said to me, "It cost twenty piasters, you rascal. You don't deserve it. Guard it like your eyes and enjoy yourself, my dear fellow."

He removed with his hand the stones that were on the ground, then took off his broadcloth cloak and spread it out along the stretch of shade and placed his turban on the stump of the branch of the mulberry tree. He lay down on the cloak, placing his right arm over his eyes, and his beard looked to me as though it were teased cotton.

"Run off," he said to me, "to where your father and uncles are and see if they've finished irrigating the Mirza field or whether they'll be spending the night in the fields."

"Right away, Grandpa. Right away."

"Tell your grandma to moisten the dates and the licorice. I'm really thirsty today."

"Right away, Grandpa."

Sleep made its stealthy way to him from the mulberry tree. He became distracted, then closed his eyes, yet he still went on talking.

"Mind you wake me before the sunset prayer, for I shall be paying a visit to the departed."

When he talked of things I didn't understand he would be on the threshold of sleep.

"Light the lantern, but beware of going to the hill of the gypsies."

His breathing became regular and his chest began moving up and down; he snored softly.

I said to myself: The hill of the gypsies—what had brought it to his mind? And why should I go there? And who would show me the way up to where the houses ended, to where one cannot walk and the wind howls in the graveyard trees?

"Beware of the hill of the gypsies. They snatch children and make tattoo marks on their chests and call them by names other than their own."

He began to dream, to talk nonsense.

I left him and went off, waving the colored lantern.

At the door I was met by my mother with her head covered. When she saw the lantern she said, "Congratulations, Abdul Mawla." I told her joyfully that my grandfather had brought it for me from the town, and she smiled at me. I said to her, "Why, when he goes to sleep, does my grandfather talk about the gypsies?" My mother said to me, "The gypsies are also God's servants—they are not to be feared." She mentioned Galeela to me and said, "And have you forgotten Galeela the gypsy, Abdul Mawla?"

"Galeela . . . Galeela." I repeated the name to myself and looked at the yellowed sun. My chest was filled with the smell of scalding milk.

Galeela the gypsy. Ah!

Three tattoo lines on her chin and the green spot to one side of her straight nose; a beauty spot like a raisin that death itself would not erase. The crescent earrings, glistening, shook when she moved her head. Eyes of divine kohl in which wandered a mysterious inscrutability. The appeal they had in the hearts of my mother and her aunts was one of life's secrets.

"We make divination in sand, we tell fortunes in sea shells. We reveal all."

"Come here, Galeela."

And on the ground of the alleyway, and under the male mulberry tree, she would spread the handkerchief and place on it the grains of soft sand. The kohl-black eye looks into the eyes of the village women, who are captivated by her hidden magic. The fingers mark out life's pathways, bringing into being the destinies of people: roads opened to good fortune, ending in weddings for virgins; peace of mind at the return of the absent. A year of bounty, udders abundant with milk, the grain stores full of the good things and the blessings of the fields. But perils, like predators, are lying in wait in the womb of the unknown, envious and hating. And the Lord is the Savior of His servants, and His Messenger a guardian, and the righteous are not harmed. And you are good and righteous, O Ameena, daughter of al-Mursi, and your son Abdul Mawla is protected from the evil eye and from the iniquities of the devils.

I listen to her voice and emerge from sleep. Passing through the door, I look for an instant into her eye, which was not the color of ashes but of light. I am pinned to the ground at the threshold, between the darkness of the house and the blaze of the sun.

Her dress is of light linen, fashioned with circles that reveal a slip the color of garden roses.

She takes me in her arms and the smell of her sweat fills me to overflowing. She says to me, "O son of the precious." I feel my head in her bosom and my heart racing madly. She kisses me on the mouth and my aunts laugh. "Leave the boy alone, you saucy wench. Sister, she's brazen and has no shame; she doesn't give a damn."

The gypsy girl laughs and my good-natured mother says to her, "Don't stay away—we miss you, Galeela." The gypsy replies, "Earning one's daily bread is full of hardship, mother of Abdul Mawla."

When she draws away from me I shudder and hear my heart beating. I see her lifting her dress and revealing the calf of her leg as she looks toward me. "Let's be seeing you, Abdul Mawla"—and she disappears in the bend of the road. Her voice carries across the valley: "We make divination, we tell fortunes in sea shells. All is revealed."

She disappears and there remains in my heart her voice and the promise that I shall see her. After the meal for breaking the fast, and drinking tea, and performing the prayer, I light the lantern. When its light is dispersed, my grandfather is delighted and he gazes at the splendor of colors spread out on the ground. I push the gate of the fence and go out into the lane.

I hear my uncle's voice warning me, "Take care of the lantern."

The lane was crowded with children and a gathering of young girls. In the houses they were busy with making pastries for the Feast, and the café radio blared out religious formulas and the glorification of God.

Seeing my lantern, the children gathered around me. They walked along behind me, their shadows falling on the ground. We went up to where the tomb of Abu Hussein stands on the canal.

"There's Sidi Abu Hussein," I shouted.

The wind roared in the high branches.

"My mother says his secret powers are fantastic and that he has performed miracles."

"And he has done favors and miracles for the whole village."

"And he sets the clouds in motion so that the rain falls."

"It's God who does that, you ignorant thing. And it's God who will raise you up on the Day of Final Judgment so that you and your father go to Hell and my grandfather and I go to Heaven."

The children laughed and looked at the lantern, whose light had grown dim. Shafika said, "The candle spluttered and the light's gone out."

"Tomorrow you'll buy a candle, Abdul Mawla, and you'll give light to the lantern."

"Tomorrow's the night of the twenty-seventh, the Night of Power."

The Night of Power, which is to say that tomorrow celestial light will be opened, prayers will be answered, and we'll go to the hill of the gypsies. I mentioned this to the children and they answered in one voice, "The hill of the gypsies? Not likely!"

They were silent, then quickly rejoined, "And why not? We'll go."

In the morning I said to my father, "Give me five piasters." And when he asked me "Why?" I said to him, "To buy a candle." He shouted at me, "And what about yesterday's candle?" I said to him, "It's finished."

Again he barked, "So, you son of your mother, you'll be wanting five piasters every day." I said, "Father, tonight's the Night of Power, and I must give light to the lantern."

My father raised the head of the ax and I screamed. I backed away and my foot sank into the mud of the cattle-pen, and I noticed the baby calf sucking at the teat of its restless mother, which was turning around on itself. I heard my grandfather's voice near the door saying to my father, "What's wrong with you?" and I heard my father reply, "By God, Father, you've brought us a real headache—he wants a candle."

He unfolded his old brown purse and undid the buttons. I could hear the click of the buttons as they were opened, and I was full of happiness. No sooner did I see the five-piaster piece than I grasped hold of His Majesty the King and heard my father shout, "That's how you'll spoil him." Then I went around all the village shops asking for a candle, from the river lane to the other side, and from the lowland right up to Marees's land. And I shouted inwardly, "What a lousy day!"

I arrived at the house shaking, and screamed at my mother, "I want a candle," and I kicked up the dust and threw a stone at the window of the upper floor. My mother stopped kneading the dough and bawled at me, "And what's got into you, Abdul Mawla? Calm down. Where do you think we'll get you a candle from?"

My uncle Ahmed shouted at me, "The devil take you, you never finish asking for things. Go up to the room on the roof and you'll find a small tin lamp, just the size of the lantern. Clean it and fix a wick in it, then fill it with oil and give us a bit of peace from your crazy idea."

I stopped crying and went up to my uncle and said to him, "And this lamp, where is it, Uncle?" He answered me, "Up above—in the window to the right of the door as you enter."

I rushed up the stairs and opened the door of the room on the roof. I searched on the window sill and came across the lamp. I found it to be old, knocked about until it was the size of a large frog. It was covered with rust and dust from being left there so long, lurking amid wooden spoons, a ball of string, old seals bearing names that had long disappeared, and contracts for land dated ages ago. I actually found a dagger with a gleaming blade inside a leather scabbard. I whispered to myself, "A dagger and a lantern."

I gathered up bolls of cotton and a complete wick, and I washed the lamp with mud and dust, and scoured it with petrol, then filled it and fitted the wick.

At night I lit the lantern and gathered the children behind me, and we hurried off to where the hill of the gypsies was. We left the village behind us and plunged into the darkness by the light of the lantern. I saw a small quantity of smoke rising up from the burning wick and blackening the sides.

We passed by the shack of Umm Bilal, that good-for-nothing woman who had no relatives. I saw her standing by her shack close to the water pump. I greeted her and she returned my greeting and asked, "Where are you off to, children?" and we replied in one voice, "To the hill of the gypsies." The woman laughed in a voice that scared us. Waving her hand at us, she called out, "The hill of the gypsies? You, you undersized, worthless lot. Go back, you naughty boys. You're not up to gypsies. If you go there they'll kidnap you and castrate you like goats. They'll open up your stomachs and take out your intestines, then fill them with salt, embalm you, and hang you up at the doors of their tents."

We were frightened, and our feet were rooted to the ground. The night around us seemed to stretch away. Said Badr made off, with Madi behind him, and they went back home.

We hastened on, penetrating deep into the night. As we walked, the light dwindled; the flame was imprisoned within the layer of soot that covered the colored glass.

A wind blew up and the trees shook. From afar, from among the graves, rose the howling of a wolf. Stars twinkled in the sky. Our voices were held captive as we clasped hands in fear.

"The worst is over, boys," I said. "The hill's close by."

I heard my voice but no reply.

The lantern's wick quivered and went out. Darkness as black as kohl descended. Shafika wept and called out, "I'm frightened."

I raised the lantern and said to them, "God will cast celestial light upon the ground."

"I want to go back."

"I shall ask of God to lengthen my grandfather's life. What will you ask of Him, Shafika?"

"I'm going home," cried out Othman, the youngest of us, and pleaded with Mongi: "Come back with me, Mongi—my mother will kill me."

The children left me and hurried back toward the village. I went on alone to my destination. In my right hand I held my lantern, whose colors had disappeared. I whispered to myself, "I'll go on by myself even if the earth be filled with devils"—and when I mentioned the devils my whole body shuddered.

The fields closed in on me and I saw the trees stretching out their branches toward me, and I heard a rustling within the alfalfa grass. I took courage and said to myself, "The devils are imprisoned in Ramadan. Calm yourself." The voice of a curlew came to me, as though saying, "Sovereignty is Yours. Sovereignty is Yours." Relaxing, I said to myself, "It is I who am wrong, I was misled by the light of the lantern going out, and that which was ordained for me"—and I walked on, following in the footsteps of the light from the stars.

I wanted to return but it was no longer possible. From afar I heard the beating of drums carried by the wind. I noticed a crescent moon, like a slice of watermelon, withdrawing into the sky. I whispered, "The hill's far away and the moon is no guide."

The hill came into view, tattooed with a few trees scattered on the sides. Three tents were illuminated by lamps attached to posts, palpitating and revealing hair tents huddled up close together.

I went up the hill. When I felt tired I sat down on a stone.

I saw them forming a circle and beating on drums and singing to the music of a flute and a reed pipe. The tune wafted to me, intimate and friendly.

I drew closer and saw the Mawawi, the chief of the gypsies, standing under the large lamp. When I looked closely I found that he had braided locks and in his left ear a silver earring, from which dangled small bells. When he raised his hands I saw that he wore on his fingers rings with bezels in the form of scarabs. Above his eyes the brows met, delineating the eyes of a hawk, while his teeth were capped with golden crowns and sparkled in the light of the gypsy fire whenever he laughed.

A gypsy of short stature moved to poke the fire with an iron prong and it blazed up. Another man had a snake, with raised head, curled about his arm; it bared its fangs and stared about it with unblinking eyes. A small monkey stood silently on his shoulder, its face expressing the wisdom found in old men.

I grew tired of looking and of my apprehensions. It was as though I had nodded off. Had I been overcome by sleep? Or had the fire, the thumping of the drums and the smiling Mawawi cast a spell over me as I saw the celestial light opening out and winged angels descending and roaming around in the place, with the perfumes of paradise being diffused? I said to myself, "I'll pray for my grandfather. On the Night of Power no prayer is left unanswered"—and I saw a gypsy greeting the angels with drums, while the Mawawi pushed his way into the circle of gypsies, taking the hand of a gypsy girl of comely face and sleek figure, clothed in a silk dress, her waist drawn in with a green belt, an end of which hung down to her thigh. She had taken up a position in the middle of the circle and had begun to dance to the rhythm of the drum. Behind her there were opened up before me gateways to flowering gardens in which the angels still circled.

"Galeela. Galeela." I called out and the Mawawi became aware of my presence. He approached me. "You came?" he said, smiling. "Ah," I said.

He drew me by the hand and I threw myself down on my back on a table. He placed his right hand on my chest and the woman with the tattoo and the crescent earrings brought the big cast-iron bowl, with the steam rising from the warm water. I whispered, "Galeela." The Mawawi asked for rosewater, ginger, saffron, camphor, and white sandalwood, and he dissolved them in the water. I heard his voice mumbling, "The letter is the origin of speech, and the Throne stands on the letter"— and I did not understand.

When I inhaled the odor of the scent, I closed my eyes and said, "Perfume." I saw him opening his knife and putting a mark on my chest, and my alarm increased. He said, "Don't be frightened," and he cleaved my chest and I groaned. Then I heard them intoning, "A speedy recovery."

I saw my heart that had been plucked out throbbing in the palm of his hand. Blood flowed from it. I heard him calling to me, "Here you are seeing your own heart." I tried to stand up, but he stopped me. He said, "Guard your secret." I said, "I'm thirsty," and he said to them, "Give him something to drink."

He placed my heart in a container and its blood floated on the water. He washed it and cleaned it and wrote letters and words on it with a reed pen, and when I asked him what he was writing he replied that he knew what he was doing.

The beating of the drums and the sounds of the flute and the reed pipe continued. Moths made their appearance above the gypsy fire, and the hill was illuminated by a heavenly resplendence.

He placed my heart in my chest and the stars that I would track until the end of my life were scattered about. I said to my grandfather, who was wearing a colored loincloth and a vast turban on his head, and clasping a scepter in his hand, "Look, Grandpa, they are my stars." But he did not look. "Debility," he said, "and long traveling is the heart's punishment." Then he placed some dates in my hand and said, before his face disappeared, "Satisfy your hunger."

The Mawawi shook me and asked me my name. Caught unawares, I forgot my name. The gypsy girl answered, "Abdul Mawla," and the Mawawi said,

"You'd gone a long way away, Abdul Mawla," and he put a candle in the lantern after washing it, and once again the colored lights of the lantern came back. He said to me, "Be careful of the stones and the runnels across the pathways. Go to your right at the next bend and you'll reach the village at daybreak."

I went down the slope of the hill and walked between the cypresses and the eucalyptus trees, inhaling the night smell of perfume and hearing the sound of singing, while to my right there gushed forth a flow of running water.

The Wolf Cub

"It's a dog, Father," I shouted. "It's a dog."

He came straight up from the canal and rested his mattock in the small watercourse.

"What would a dog be coming to you for, boy?" he said.

I was standing by the stable for the water buffalo and the donkey under the solitary male date palm, gazing at that strange animal as it looked at me with unblinking eyes.

When my father came up to me, tying the end of his gown around his middle, his legs bespattered with mud, and with sweat on his forehead, he stopped and regarded what I had thought was a dog.

"That's no dog, boy," he said. "That's a young wolf that's lost its mother."

My heart beat fast. I was amazed as I looked at that thing sitting on its haunches and pricking its ears as it gazed boldly toward us. It had a wide forehead and its fur was brown, while its eyes gave out a dazzling brilliance. I was imagining its mother crossing the fields in search of it.

"I'll bring it up, Father," I said, "and it'll be like a dog which is half wolf."

A turtledove circled in the sky and alighted near the wolf. When it gave a growl, the dove soared off into the western sky.

27

I was standing on the threshold of my discovery, looking in disbelief at what I'd found, while the wolf stared back at me with eyes full of deep enmity. I approached it to pick it up and the enmity in its eyes turned to fear. It cowered below the trunk of the date palm and made a strange whimpering sound. I stretched out my hand to pick it up and it started back, the hair on its head standing up, and it bared its small fangs and growled. I was frightened of it but my father gave me a prod in the side and shouted angrily at me, "Get going, boy. No one's scared of a young wolf."

I took it up and it wriggled and scratched me on the arm, so I let it go and it fell with a bump to the ground and began yelping. Then it ran off between the lines of crops. However, I caught it and brought it back.

My father smiled and said, "Enjoy yourself, man. By God, you've got yourself a dog which is the son of a wolf."

My father finished his irrigation work and untied the buffalo from the waterwheel. Winding its leading-rope around its neck, he let it loose. He put me onto the donkey and I went off behind the buffalo, carrying the wolf against my chest. It had calmed down and had allowed itself to be made captive without me having to use any force.

In the village the children said to me, "Who'd think of bringing up a wolf?"

"Yes, me," I said to them.

"You've gone off your head, boy," they said to me. "It'll eat you."

"Not it, it won't—when it's brought up with us it'll get used to us."

"Get used to who, man?" they said. "That's a wolf, a child of the open country. Keeping it shut up will kill it."

My uncle had told me the story of Ibrahim al-Areeni, who used to work with us as a day laborer. At the end of each day he would wander off into the night to sleep near where the water was. One dawn, he arranged his place for sleeping and stretched out on the track of the waterwheel and began snoring. After a while he woke up to find something heavy squatting on his chest. Coming to, he found for sure that a wolf the size of a large sheep was sitting quietly on his heart and staring up in the direction of the moon. The day laborer was scared out of his wits and was convinced that he was about to meet the Face of his Maker, and that after a moment the wolf would tear his ribs apart and, with due permission of the One God, he would meet a sudden and violent death. Al-Areeni said, "I take refuge in God from the accursed Devil," and then, "There's only one life and only One Lord." With this he deftly moved his hand so that he could grasp the handle of the serrated sickle by his side. Then, with all determination, a determination created by fear, he struck out with the sickle and pierced the eye of the beast. The weapon, with a thrust inspired by fear and with the help of the Almighty, lodged itself in the animal's head. It rushed off in terror, blundering about in the mud of the water channels, howling in the half light of dawn, while Ibrahim al-Areeni, out of his mind, darted away, peeing in his pants and shouting, "Help! Come to my rescue!"

When it was daylight the men came back and found the wolf a lifeless carcass, half of it sunk in the drainage canal and the other half on the bank, with the sickle blade stuck in its eye. At that moment Ibrahim al-Areeni stepped forward, tore it out from the beast's eye, and used it to slit open the animal and snatch out its heart, which he devoured raw in front of everyone.

They say in our village that whoever eats the heart of a wolf will never know fear in his own heart. And so al-Areeni lived without knowing fear until he was bitten by a rabid wolf, when he died howling and tied to the trunk of a tree which gave shade to his house on the borders of the distant open country.

In front of our house was a reed shack under the shade of a willow, a casuarina, and a male mulberry tree that had been there from time immemorial. Our house marked the last of the village, skirted on the east by the river and with the gristmill to the west, and in front of it the magnificent fields opening out as far as the eye could see until you reached the beginning of the desert, the open country, where the sands began and ended at the great sea.

The winds blow and I hear the casuarina, the mulberry, and the willow talking with the words of the wind. I am frightened and I lie on my bedding with sleep eluding me as I try to drive away a thousand and one afreets.

I had tied the wolf to a thin metal chain and had put around its neck a brown piece of decorated leather, and I had fixed it to a stake by the reed shack. I put in front of it my portion of the meat from supper and the bones that were left from the table and an earthenware pot of milk from the evening's milking. I waited for it to eat. It was crouching under the wall, taking refuge from me in its banishment. It felt lonely in this unfamiliar place and among strange people, and it yearned for the faraway deserts, the open spaces of the mountains, the voice of the winds, and the lairs of its ancestors.

It scorned food and drink and looked hostilely in my direction.

I stamped with my foot and closed the door, saying to myself, "Once it's hungry it'll eat whether it likes it or not."

At night, at the end of the night, I heard its howling.

It was a long, drawn-out howling that brought a shudder of fear to my body, a howling that made its way from the reed shack, pierced through the built-up area and reached the distant fields, as though answering sounds I did not hear. I was frightened of going to sleep in case I should find it sitting on my chest. I got up, gazed out of the window, and saw the moon looking down with wide-open eyes and the wind blowing coldly and with the smell of growing crops and flowing waters.

The howling again gave answer to the moon. I heard a scratching at the shack door and the whimpering of the captive animal.

"It'll be worn out by tiredness and will go to sleep," I said to myself and slept.

In the morning it had not gone near the food and had not slept. I looked closely at its eyes and found in them something that resembled fever.

In the field my uncle said to me, "Son, wolves hate being shut up."

"It'll get used to it," I said.

"Son," he said, "I didn't sleep the whole night because of the wolf's howling. It was as if . . . as if it was calling to its mother. Let it go, son, and you'll get your reward from God. Your Lord created such animals free."

"No way," I said.

He looked in my direction and strode off toward the far end of the land, and I heard him muttering, "As stubborn as his father."

On the third night I heard it scratching at the door and biting at the chain. It seemed to be attacked by a fit of madness. Whenever the moon was shining brightly it would give vent to its howling. I would look down and see it through the small aperture at the bottom of the wall of the shack. It was lunging from one wall to the other, choked by the sensation of being imprisoned. Whenever the sound of the wind, coming from far-off deserts, grew louder, its howling intensified.

I went down from my room and opened the front door. I waded through the belly of the moon, which was at its fullest. I heard a shot in the fields, and the wolf went berserk as it breathed in from afar the smell of what had been shot.

On opening the shack door, I saw its eyes glistening like two live coals, as bright as fire. The way the eyes shone and the bared teeth, and the hostility with which the animal faced me, were frightening.

At dawn the howling ceased, also the striking at the reeds and the scratching at the chain.

In the morning I opened the shack door. The small animal of the open wastes was stretched out dead. Blood had dripped down from its wounded lips, its claws too were stained with blood, while its head protruded through a small opening in the wall of the shack. Its eyes, wide-open, stared out with the hope of escape toward the openness where lay the fields and the distant wastelands.

The Boy on the Bridge

There it is, fixed high above the door of the house, with its two wings outspread, covered with the dust of ages, and its voracious red beak aimed toward the salty earth soggy with refuse and the remnants of tattered objects. (Who had brought it from faraway lands and driven nails into its wings, there in the face of the sun? I didn't know, I that boy who was baffled by the alphabet of things.)

My father told me that my grandfather had caught it, that he had brought it back after the passage of the seasons and that my grandfather had imprisoned it in the top room of the house. The bird had not stopped wailing and had kept flapping its fabulous wings in the empty space of the room, and they would hear the rushings of air and be frightened. At that time I had not yet been born. Things were not as they are now and our house was on the very edge of the village and was surrounded by ever-green olive trees, with an inner garden that gave fruit throughout the year regardless of the seasons. Nearby was an old-fashioned waterwheel made of wood; it had ceased to draw up water and had become a signpost to the place and the house. I was drawn to the bird, without knowing whether it was alive or dead. My father told me that on the day my grandfather died the bird had died, and I did not believe him. He also told me that they never saw a bird like it and that they did not know in which country it had been caught. Whenever I walked through into the house I would sense its presence above my head; its wailing would reverberate in my heart, and vast stretches of trees in the night would be draped in a darkness like that of the wells dug at the ends of the world. I would set out on my own, passing between the trees, straying from the road as I searched for it with childish stubbornness and a frantic desire to take hold of it. I would see it in the distance, that bird with the voracious red beak, unfolding its wings among the stars. In its wild flight its eyes would be fixed on mine. I would be afraid of it, and propping myself against the trunk of one of the ancient trees, I would weep—and my mother would wake me from my dreams.

I walked along the garden path by the edge of the well that had been dug beside the wall. It was springtime. The density of the vegetation and its leafy shadows were tracing disturbingly irregular shapes on the wall. My big brother was standing beside the pump, whose ground was sodden with muddy waste water. I said to him, "I've seen a bird like it." Looking at me sharply with an inquiring glance, he asked me what bird I meant. I said, "The one that's over there." He went up the flight of steps, turning his back on me. His shadow was preceding him and the prickly branches of the trees were stretching across the wall. Standing and looking in my direction, my brother told me I should not waste my time. I came up close until I was right behind him and I shouted out at him that he would see when I brought it and imprisoned it in the top room and I could hear its wailing as my grandfather had done. My brother laughed and entered the house.

Alone I stand between the shade and the sun. Behind me is the wall and in front of me the door through which looms the crouched waterwheel, behind it the river, while the gusts of the *khamseen* winds whirl around.

I was roaming about every day and not finding it. I made my own times and festivals. I walked warily in the place and took cover in the shade and by the trunks of trees. I conversed with the river, the crops, the moon, and the mausoleum. In my dreams I grasped it and in daylight it flew from me. I grew sad and experienced the meaning of weeping and fear. Many winds blew and I saw pass by me many of the boats that were sailing to distant ports. I would see their white sails spread and fill with wind, giving out a sound like the beating of drums, and I would hear their sailors singing and would know that they were unhappy. My father had said to me, "That was a different age: the men were different, the time different." He told me that at the time he was older than I was by several years and that his mustache had not yet begun to grow. Only a few people walked in the land and you would not meet a soul. They used to be over there, gathered in a circle around the heaped-up fire that loomed over their heads. Behind them was the mausoleum and beyond it stretched the graveyards right up to their known boundary. And at a distance, the village, ancient and immersed in darkness, lay sprawled. They were surrounding the person known as the man from Java, who had come from faraway lands, his complexion different from ours, his appearance different; coming with his strangely fashioned clothes, which were generally black, while hanging from his neck were necklaces in a thousand colors and shapes. On his back he would be carrying his bag of provisions, while in his hand he held his hooked stick. He would rap at our door with his stick and call out to my grandfather, his voice rising to the top rooms and stealing its way into the house like an echo: "Get up, Abdul Ghaffar—the man from Java has arrived." My grandfather would drowsily rise and dress hastily, while my grandmother would seat herself on the edge of the bed. My grandfather would call out: "Welcome to the noble one, the son of the noble. The times of blessings and good fortune have come."

Over there the sun is going down. I see it from my position on top of the bridge. The sun was departing, leaving behind it the eternal lake of blood, while the fragrance of the day's end—the smell of water and shore plants—was being diffused. I saw the ancient sycamore with its vast bulk embedded in the earth of the area of my quest, around which walked the animal that drove the waterwheel. The tree gave no shade at sunset, its arms extended to where the road lies along which God's creatures have been returning in autumnal ranks for thousands of years. I skirted around the sycamore

and above my head there flashed past a flight of
pigeons returning to their dovecotes. From afar
there came to me the sound of the call to evening
prayers stealing over the water and carving deep
fear into my chest. I would remember those who
had died: that grandfather of mine whom I used to
see at the end of his days supporting his weight on
his hooked stick, sitting in front of the gate of the
house's spacious garden from spring to autumn,
looking in my direction with his tired eyes and
calling out to me, "You son of a dog, no one lasts.
Life cannot be a companion." I used not to
understand what he was saying. I would watch his
footsteps that had grown heavy and would thrust
myself under his shoulder so he could lean on me.

(O bird who has strayed from its nest, here I am
awaiting you.)

There they were alone, their arms dangling on
legs that had been drawn up. The graveyards were
scattered, the abodes of memories and forefathers.
On their walls were ranged pieces of marble on
which were dates and names. People I did not
know passed through the narrow openings of
graves; the passageways between them were
covered with soft earth. Swarms of blue flies
buzzed with the setting of the sun as they searched
for apertures to shelter in. Mastic, casuarina, and
eucalyptus trees with their ancient intimate sounds.
The large teapot, variegated with colors like henna,
with my father standing behind the mound of wheat
that knelt camel-like on the floor of the barn; my
grandfather alongside the man from Java, the

worker of miracles, his old bag of provisions positioned beside him, with his white beard, the badge of righteousness and piety, and his way of expressing himself that was so easily understood by heart and soul. They loved him greatly. "Listen, Hagg Abdul Ghaffar. No one has vanquished time. I am eighty years of age. I have traveled far and wide. Now the grave is catching up with me." At night, cold breezes blow and the fires die, leaving behind their ashes, while at their stalls the animals chew the cud with a monotonous, comforting sound. All are slumbering and time holds sway, as though it is the little death of sleep that is in charge. The devils come screaming in the trees with a thunderous rumble, then they make their way on the night dust toward the sea. And in sleep come the good spirits in place of the day's toil. (In the beleaguered silence comes the sound of the strange bird, diffused, neither a glorification nor a singing but something resembling a wailing.)

Were I now to walk for an hour I would be at the bridge. There, at the crossways at this time of the year, the river would be plunging headlong, feeding the mud banks and revivifying the wild plants in bloom. I had said to my brother, "I know where its nest is"—and I was lying. My clothes were blue as the sky and my mind had not yet matured. I had said to my grandfather that I would give him the sun, and he had said to me from a mouth devoid of teeth that he must be watchful and on his guard against becoming drowsy near the well. And when I told him I would bring the bird from the bank of the canal, he had looked toward me and said he did not understand anything. I said to my brother that once I had seen it at the place by the river's edge where the women cleaned the pots of an afternoon; and it was where the many white birds were congregating on the branches of the sycamore tree, those birds that resembled a vast tent, and their voices came to me with the sound of the waters. It was there, with its brown color shading into blueness and its voracious red beak: that same bird of mine that was hanging on the door of the house. I ran toward it and climbed the tree warily, and all the birds became frightened and flapped their wings in the air as they made off. I reached it and, looking toward it, said, "O bird with the large eyes, don't raise your voice and don't fly off with your wings and cast me again into confusion. Stay where you are and I shall stretch out my hand now to take you." I was frightened that it would fly off with me, but I stretched out my hand to seize hold of it by the fan of feathers, but it had flown off, disappearing into space.

Every day I would come to the bridge; the sun would disappear and I would return disappointed, until that last morning came.

At the top of the bridge was a public watering fountain built by some Mameluke of old for merit and heavenly recompense. Its colors were still resplendent and it had some writing on it in corroded, unintelligible letters; it had a high dome and its water was always cold, quenching the thirst of wayfarers and field laborers. Also, there was the hut of the policeman on patrol, who comes only with the night, and a place of kilns for baking bricks, from which issued the familiar smell resembling that of earthenware pots of milk in ovens. A line of eucalyptus trees, another mulberry, and shadows. An afternoon nap undisturbed by any footsteps, lanes that are deserted, a doze in a weary day. I alone am above the bridge, my eyes cleaving to God's vast space, my head turning in the redness of noon.

The sun flashes at noon, bright and inflamed; it holds sway. My eyes search the tops of the trees and above the dovecotes and on the earth of the patches of unirrigated land. The earth is an open space for time, and the sky a pasture for the inflamed sun.

(If only I were to catch sight of you now, O bird!)

I said this and leaned on the iron railing of the bridge and conversed with my grandfather: I spoke to him about time and its passing. He talked to me about the endings of life and he did not smile. But there it was, circling around itself in the vastness of space, there with its two wings spread out like a fan, its red beak and its unblinking eyes, determining the place where it would alight from its remote height. (I know you, the man from Java knows you, and my grandfather used to know you.) Whenever the man from Java was bewitched by the night and had spent a long time scrutinizing the moon and had seen the Lord's creatures calling him, he would take up his hooked stick and put his provisions bag over his shoulder and follow the voices that did not stop calling him, and it was only after the elapse of many years that he would return.

I saw the bird alighting with its weight at its place on the high branch of the sycamore tree, giving the final flap of its wings, spreading them out to the full, and coming to rest on the branch. The branch was exposed to the sky. It alighted on it alone, moving its head toward where the sun rises.

I saw a man making his way stealthily from the dense thickets. He was wearing a leather jacket and had a hat on his head; on his shoulder he had a pale khaki-colored cloth bag and he was carrying a gun with a long barrel. The hunter stared at the bird and took aim. The bird was within range. (Now the bullet will be fired and will shoot forth, convulsing the blazing silence of midday; the exposed breast will be rent and the bird will fall, stained with its blood, the flesh of the belly ripped apart, the voracious red beak thrust into the dust.) I said to my grandfather that nothing lasts and he told me that things appear similar to a frightening degree when the time comes. I gave a shout that was like a call for help. The bird flew off and circled as it watched the hunter, who was again taking aim. The bird plunged down from its resplendent height, spreading its claws like spears: it was going straight for the face of the hunter, who had suddenly become frightened. The spear-like claws thrust themselves into the face, wrenching out the eyes with primordial savagery. The gun was on the ground and the hands flailing at the air, while the face turned in its sudden blindness, and plaintive screams exploded in the heat of midday. The bird was soaring, vanishing into unconfined space, as I stood on the bridge gazing at what I was seeing and understanding nothing.

The Camel, Abdul Mawla, the Camel!

The boy of good fortune mounts the she-ass (he did not know he would be meeting it). He rides off from the west of the field right up to the pathway. The world—in his dream—reveals itself as a twinkling star, with the sun standing right overhead, where he sees it making its way with sails of fire, appearing, as it leaves him, as an affliction to the heart.

As he stood there, two moons passed over him, and thirty suns in which blew a wind pleasant to begin with but blazing and treacherous with the last of the suns.

He does not know what induced him to wait.

(It was as though he was expecting it to appear.)

It looms slyly in the noonday space, bringing anxieties to his heart.

A long neck of bones and fur, ending in a small delicate head with two frighteningly wide eyes.

(I was not able to contend against them, so I fled from my fear by shielding my eyes so I should not see what I was seeing.)

A lip that had been split as though struck by a knife gathers the greenness of twigs from the tops of trees, which are then chewed by teeth like the grains of corncobs.

(If only I had not mounted the she-ass and quit the west side of the field and had stayed on watching the fish's eyes that stared at me from the brook and which appeared to be smiling; if only I had not been so rash as to leave my mother who waits for me from first daylight on the threshold, putting her hand to her eye and gazing into the distance and asking herself, "What's delayed the boy?")

It pushes its arched neck against the adobe wall. It collapses, the dust rising up like smoke. It makes a way for itself through which it can penetrate in search of the boy.

It appeared with its large body on the lane, hurrying along, and a covey of sand grouse flitted past with a whir of wings in the direction of the water.

(It searches for me, hurries after me, rushing along with its four hooves that leave imprints in the dust. Whenever I look in its direction my heart quakes and all peace of mind leaves me. It comes out from between the trees and makes for me, while I am as though fettered to the donkey's back, which has grown stubborn and refuses to budge. I hear its gurglings like a drum in the emptiness of the red-hot noonday.)

(The camel of the house—there's our camel.)

He let it out as a cry for help, a reverberating scream.

"Help—the camel of the house is going to kill me."

He awoke from his dream to an instant of wakefulness, that wakefulness that is half sleep and half consciousness. He felt a hand being placed on his forehead. Was it that of Madawi, his sister who sleeps beside him? Or the hand of his tender mother, Ameena?

He heard a voice he did not recognize: "May the Prophet's name guard you and keep you safe. The boy's dreaming."

It was necessary for him to come back from the moment of waking, that moment that was half sleep and half consciousness, so as to see that thing with the hooves and the tall hump coming toward him with ordered power.

He left the donkey and made for the bridge, running under a naked sky, with the camel staring at him and the distance between them narrowing. The boy had the impression that he had become paralyzed, that his foot was stuck in a plantation of rice that had been irrigated.

"The camel's going to kill me."

He fervently hoped to see some human being, a man by the river. Turning off to the right, he passed through the line of *sant* trees and the orange grove and crossed the bridge. He heard in the distance—in his dream—the sound of the call to prayer coming from the mosque of Abu Hussein, and he hurried off in its direction.

His foot slipped and he fell, supporting himself on his hand. He was aware of the camel's footsteps and its heavy breathing on the back of his neck. No more than a few inches separated him from his pursuer.

He was surprised to find Sidi Abu Hussein himself standing at the door of the mosque.

"Sidi Abu Hussein." He said it with yearning, his hand outstretched like someone in want.

He manifests himself in a cloak of blue broadcloth, on his head a vast turban with a green shawl around it the color of the crops, his face encircled by a white beard of venerable length.

"Come to my rescue, my lord—the camel's going to kill me."

(When I had thrown myself into Sidi's arms, my panic left me, and when I looked toward the camel I found it standing in its place. The moment Sidi had motioned to the camel "Stay where you are, camel," the camel had come to a stop where it was and had wept.)

In the morning he told his mother his dream.

He told her that he was afraid of sleeping in case he dreams and sees the camel.

She placed her hand on his chest and said to him, "I'll make a vow for you and give to the poor—and the camel in dreams is a sheikh."

He told her that for a long time he had been seeing the camel in dreams and that he had come to hate their own camel and all the camels in the village.

She said, "Let's make good the vow and give something to charity, then the fear will go away."

In the afternoon she made ready the colored rush basket decorated with pictures of dolls and she placed in it the offerings of fulfillment of her vow.

Rounds of cake, oranges, and—the bounty of His goodness—a pastry made of tip-top flour, and into

her pocket she thrust a pound for the sheikh, and
on the road from the village to the tomb of the saint
she said a prayer, "O Abu Hussein, here are your
offerings. Remove from my boy his fear, for fear in
the village is a characteristic of women."

The boy, having crossed the Rubat bridge, seated
himself on the stone wall, raising his knee and
resting his chin on it, staring out at the dirt road and
seeing at a distance a long line of camels coming in a
mixed batch, tied head to tail, on their way to the
Tuesday market. He saw their high shanks
descending on the track, and their saliva flowing
down in strings to the ground. He rises from where
he is sitting and addresses himself to the owner of
the camels, "Where are you off to?" The man looks
at him in surprise and answers, "To market."

He continues to stare at the troop of camels
going on until they vanish from sight, while in his
head the dream camel assumes concrete form.

His dream is repeated several times.

At night he is frightened, and the neighbors, male
and female, are frightened and come to the house.

Sakeena has informed the women of the dream
and they have told her that the father of Abdul
Mawla himself must make a vow to give some big
offerings, that the man is greedy and would sell his
own grandmother. Sakeena bawled at the women,
telling them to shut up, and telling them that the
man gives money away in alms and is God-fearing
and treats people in a way that is pleasing to God.
The poor have a share in his wealth, but the truth of

the matter is that the boy is the victim of the evil eye.

When the father was riding off on the back of the donkey, making twists of clover and pushing them into the side of the camel's mouth, which was like the maw of an oven, Hagg Yusuf Obeid passed by riding on his donkey. After exchanging greetings he asks, "What's wrong with the boy?"

"He's fine."

"A bit simple-minded?"

"Not at all. It's just some trouble that will pass. He's frightened."

"God is the Rescuer."

He tapped the neck of the donkey with the stick and drove his right foot into its side and gave out a "Haa" in a hoarse voice so that the donkey broke into a run, trailing a cloud of fine dust that rose as high as the father and his camel, which he then began to address in an audible voice.

"Now don't think yourself as a sheikh. How long are you going to go on frightening my boy? Take it easy with my son and don't give me yet more worries, for the treasures of the earth would not compensate me for an idiot boy."

The camel brayed and turned away its head. It looked down on the father from on high, and the father said resignedly, "It's destiny, it's foreordained."

In the forenoon they set traps for the sand grouse and threw stones at the jujube fruit and picked up some of the grapes from Abdul Ghani Badr's field that had already been garnered, and they saw boats on the river traveling with earthenware jars and a cargo of sugar cane.

In Abu Musa's prayer room they took off their clothes, and threw themselves into the river. They swam to the other shore and back, then got out of the water. A boy called out at Abdul Mawla, "They say you're frightened of the camel."

"In dreams."

"You mother's boy, no one's afraid of a camel."

"The camel's an enemy."

"The fact is you're a coward and the son of a coward."

When he did not find his clothes, he asked the children, "Where are my clothes?" and they laughed at him and gathered around him as he stood there naked. He was in the center of them, his genitals and backside in view. "My clothes, you sons of bitches!" he screamed at them, but all they did was to make fun of him in a noisy procession, shouting "Chomp, camel, chomp, chomp, chomp, camel, chomp."

At night he choked in his sleep. His mother got up and borrowed from the neighbor the special shallow metal bowl against the evil eye for him to drink out of so that he might be protected. She put it out on the roof with its water until the morning. When he got up he drank it, and that same night the camel attacked him.

Friday noon his aunt came to the house. She was the woman in whose arms he would seek refuge, the woman he treated just like his mother.

They entered the reception room, in which was diffused a slight murkiness, and he heard her calling to his mother, "The fire, Ameena."

His mother came in carrying the earthenware container with a pyramid of corncobs arranged on it, all well alight so that they burned as red as the eye of an afreet. His mother placed the fire in the middle of the space where the steps led upstairs. She threw some incense into it and a fragrant smell rose up, a smell that reminded her of the sheikh's tomb.

He was sitting alongside the wall, his hand tucked into the inside of his gallabiya, waiting. He heard his aunt talking to herself: "The heart's troubles won't leave us, and some have more troubles than others."

"The doll, Ameena."

He saw a paper doll with two arms and legs spread open, and a rounded head. He saw his mother pierce the eye and body of the doll with a needle, while his aunt muttered strange invocations over him, boldly appealing to God for help as though she saw Him close by. "Take away from my son his fear, for we are people who have no quarrel with anyone."

As he stepped over the fire the first time she muttered, "The first is in the name of God." He stepped over it a second time and he heard her say, "And the second is in the name of God." He stepped a third time and he heard her say, "And the third time is in the name of God," until he did so for the seventh time, when he heard her say, "And in

the seventh I invoke protection for you from the
eye of someone who is envious and who, when he
saw you, didn't pronounce His name."

She threw some salt into the corners of the room
and stuck the paper doll into the mud wall. The
scorching heat spread through the place, while
through the open window his aunt's voice reached
to outside.

(And I was amid the smoke, frightened of my
aunt and my mother. I seek the protection of the
wall. Looking out of the window, I see it in front of
me, chewing the cud with steady composure,
staring fixedly in my direction as though it had
come in answer to the smell of the incense, the
mumblings, and the incantations. It glared at me for
a long time and I let out a scream. My aunt and
mother grasped what had happened and looked out
of the window. "The camel . . . the camel!" they
called out. It was without a leading rope and was
moving its jaws in a regular, monotonous manner,
looking in our direction. I was raising my gown in
terror and exposing my genitals as I started back
from the suffocating smoke and the sudden sight of
the camel.)

My aunt seized hold of a handful of ashes and
threw them into the camel's face as she shouted at
it, "Leave us alone, you accursed thing—the boy's
our only child."

The next morning he went around with his father.

The man took him up to where the camel was
stabled and said to him, "Look, Abdul Mawla, the

camel does no harm." He tried to get up close to it, but he was frightened.

His father did not want to put any pressure on him, so he left him and went off to the far end of the land.

He played around the stable but was careful not to go near to where it was. He chased after a butterfly that was flitting about, but failed to catch it.

He glanced in the direction of the camel. It was standing bolt upright under the date-palm, its neck stretched out at a level with the shack built in the stable yard.

He saw it freeing itself from its fetter, uprooting the stake to which it was tied. It set off, crossing the bridge with its gray body, its tall back empty of its wooden saddle.

The boy, taken by surprise, stared at it and took to his heels, making for the drainage canal bridge, with the camel following him.

"Save me, father!"

He rushed forward at a run, the huge frame racing after him, with the hooves making a sound like when the bat beats out the dough.

Abdul Mawla was panting: his breathing labored, his heart beating against his chest, staring into the empty space that stretched in front of him, aware of the disaster chasing after him.

"Come and rescue me, father—the camel, the camel!"

"The nose-ring!" his father shouted at him. "Pull the nose ring, Abdul Mawla, and stand your ground."

The boy's urine trickled down between his thighs and the camel gave a bellow as the distance between them narrowed.

"Stand where you are, boy."

(I stood there with my heart beating. As it drew closer the urine flowed down from me. Then I felt something unknown to me rise up from my heart to my hand, something that made me call out "There's only one life and only one God"—and I faced up to the camel. My aim was to get hold of the nose-ring. I grasped it and pulled with all the strength of those who are afraid. The camel backed away, while I drew it forward; it struggled and tossed its head as it tried to drag me along. But the noose of fire through its nose, and the jerking movements of my hand, made it submit with grumbling roars.

In a broken voice the camel wept and wailed. I saw its spittle flowing down its cheek, and I saw my father running toward me with his mattock in his hand. When he saw the camel letting out its roaring noises, he said to me, "Make it kneel. Make it kneel.")

When he had made the camel kneel and stand up again, then kneel again and stand up, Abdul Mawla drew it along behind him. He was carrying the branch from a mulberry tree in his hand and was lifting it up in front of the camel's eye. Under his bare feet he could feel the hot dust of the road, while the father looked on at what had happened in disbelief.

The Night Book

There wasn't a young boy of my age who did not wish to belong to the Islamic Group in that far-off time.

Believe me, this is what happened to me:

The Group had their place in a narrow alley, on both sides of which were cavernous houses; there was also a mulberry tree whose age went back to our forefathers and in which we used to play during the day. The alley ended in a small dome, like the nipple of a breast, covering the tomb of a saint of whose origin we knew nothing, not even from what country he came.

The Emir of the Group would bring us together during the day and at night, when he would sort us into families, each family consisting of four boys, with one of our own age being put in charge. Each family would bear the name of one of the revered Companions of the Prophet, with my own family having the name of Abu Dharr al-Ghifari, the patron and ally of the poor.

The Emir would gather us on the top floor to recite to him the prophetic Traditions we had learned by heart. On the walls of the meeting-place were verses from the Holy Koran and a photograph of the General Guide dressed in a cloak and wearing a tarboosh, his face encircled by a beard which gave him a venerable appearance. The Emir would point at the photograph with the words, "This is our Guide and the person in charge of your welfare. If you have obeyed him, you will go to heaven; if you have disobeyed him, you will be destined for Hell-fire—and may God save us from that!"

I lived all my life in fear that the Guide would push me into Hell-fire.

For a whole month I had learned no more than a single Tradition. When my turn came, the Emir would ask me to recite. I would stand up straight, stretch out my neck, deepen my voice and say, "He said, may blessings and peace be upon him: Do not be angry."

With these words I would escape by the skin of my teeth from being punished. Each time I would say "Do not be angry" until the Emir became fed up and screamed at me, "You little devil, don't you know any Tradition but 'Don't be angry,' when there are so many of them?"

Then he brought his cane down mercilessly on my small body while I screamed out, "Please, sir — honestly I'll learn them." But he went on beating me until my body was black and blue, and I was struck dumb by grief and silent tears.

From that day I hated the Emir, though not the Group. He would come to me in my dreams in the form of an afreet and I would start up from the depths of sleep in terror and would find comfort only in my mother's embrace.

At dawn the Emir would take us to swim in the cold waters of the river. As I dived down into the darkness, I would shake with fear at the feeling that tens of genies were living there and that they would draw me down and plunge me into faraway depths. After our swimming session, we would settle down in the open-air camp. We would make a fire at night and recite the Koran in our young voices, surrounded by silence and open spaces under a sky marked by clouds.

After Friday prayers the Emir would gather the Group together and would settle himself in our midst with his tall body and gaze at us with that one-eyed look I hated; I hated, too, his horrible way of behaving, not least of which being the way he would poke us in the side with his pointed stick and it would feel as though it had gone right in. Our venerable Emir said, "There's a book buried under al-Saheeti's sycamore tree on the river bank and it must be brought here an hour before dawn, and I choose for this task the young devil, Ibn Salama."

I peed on myself and could feel the warm flow between my thighs, sure that a catastrophe had befallen me. "Al-Saheeti's sycamore tree, God help me!" I said to myself. "I'm scared to go there even in daytime."

The sycamore tree crouched like some animal over there by the river, the abode of afreets and robbers and those that had been drowned; it was well known in the village that genies would emerge from the water at night and hold their festivities and weddings underneath it, when there would be a blowing of woodwinds and a beating of drums as they searched after human prey.

My mouth went dry and beads of sweat broke out on my body as I became sure that the Emir was singling me out. How was I, as young as I was, going to be able to walk alone through the dead of night that is so feared by birds, beast, and man, to arrive at that place where one's fate awaits one? I wanted to say "Me . . . me?" but he interrupted me with the words: "And what's up with you? You scared?" I remained silent, embarrassed in front of the young boys to show I was frightened, so I answered him, "Just as you say." At this he shouted at me, "You'll take yourself off and bring back the book from there. Understood?"

I walked stumblingly across the embankment in the suffocating night, with the trees standing there like giants and the darkness thickening below them. It seemed to me I could hear voices whispering words whose meaning I did not know. At that time and in that terrifying open space I became sure that fear possessed another meaning and sense than that of my fear when I was sleeping.

A wind blew from the direction of the river as I made my way, shrunk in upon myself like some worn-out old garment. Whenever I heard the sound of fish jumping in the water or of the desert hawks crossing God's high heavens, I would glance around me in terror.

When I arrived at the sycamore tree, I had lost half of myself through fear, and I was cursing the Emir and his merciless treatment of me. Shadows were stretched out under the sycamore like a black robe.

I dug under the roots with my nails, the taste of the earth in my nostrils. Not finding the book, I was afraid to break out crying as I realized how alone and helpless I was. When my hand caught hold of the book, I was overjoyed and felt that it was some God-given gift.

As I brought it out and pulled it from its cloth wrapping, I was conscious of footsteps making their way stealthily toward me. When I looked toward where they came from, I found a giant dressed in black, with only two eyes showing that gleamed in the darkness. My knees shook and I was paralyzed with fear. Instead of collapsing where I stood, I at once took to my heels.

I was running across the embankment as swiftly as a pigeon, the tail of my gown clenched in my teeth, and the book clutched to me, calling out at the top of my voice, "An afreet. . . an afreet!"

The afreet itself was running right behind me and it too was shouting, "Stop boy. I'm the Emir—I'm Sheikh Mahmoud al-Damrani."

I didn't believe him and kept on running along the embankment, taking into my lungs what breath I could and wiping the sweat from my brow. I was possessed by a sort of ox-like stubbornness and the overwhelming sensation that this book was my property and that no one in the whole world had the right to wrest it from me—not the world, nor my father, nor the Emir himself. I put on more speed as the footsteps tried to catch up with me, footsteps that beat down on the sand of the embankment like hammers.

After this I gave up belonging to the Group, though until today the book is still in my possession.

A Matter of Honor

The lamp east of the village, with a divine light, traces shadows on the place, the twist of the river, the distant burial grounds.

A heavy slumber before the downpour of the first beams of light, and a cold rap from the early morning air. The sound of coughs and the dripping of water from the taps in the ablution fountain at the mosque of the saint Abu'l-Makarim, west of the village.

An odor is brought by the wind from the caves that lie far from where any building stands, and from the shabby rooms open to the night the scandal was spread from abroad, with the sobbing of the sorrowing, and the smell of the milking rooms, and the diffusion of the smell of the first morning's bread from ovens blazing with fire, and the mud of the cattle folds, and the wormwood used for keeping snakes away, and the incense employed in incantations, and the semen of unlawful lusts in threadbare trousers, and the tears in the eyes of solitary widows, separated by death and lengthy travel.

Animals in foal or in labor, others sterile and awaiting the knives of the slaughterers and butchers, and a woman whose hand rests on the window of the saint's tomb complaining with tearful eyes of the sterility of her womb and her longing for children, the first scream of the newly born, and the rattling of brass containers at the ceremony for the seventh day after birth.

"A new morning by the Lord's grace."

A morning like a thousand mornings. A disgrace has been revealed and the world on this accursed morn has come into being.

The pretty girl, a girl with a background, a girl from a decent family, with a complexion as white as cream and eyes the color of clover, with her two blond plaits under a blue shawl. She stands, hidden by the iron bridge, wearing an embroidered silk dress. Round her neck are two chains, one of silver with a heart and the other of gold ending in some verses from the Holy Book.

The bridge joins the village to the provincial center. Its heart beats once in the morning and once in the evening when it opens out to allow the passage of boats laden with sand and cargoes of sugar cane and white pitchers. They leave the place accompanied by the singing of folk songs and the odor of distant countries. The heart of the bridge beats and prepares to meet the tread of human beings and the hooves of animals.

The girl has been standing there from early night, frightened of where she's going and of knocking at the door of her family, she who is impure, she who has given herself to illicit love, and who has left her village in flight behind him whom her heart has chosen, that man of the town who deserted her after a time. He left her alone, while she gazed at faces in the city in the hope that she might come across his absent face.

"I see them as though they are emerging from my ribs: my grandfather the omda, my grandmother the grand lady, and my mother with her dejected appearance, who, throughout the time I was away, used to stand by her window looking out westward, awaiting the coming of night with a heavy heart."

Shafak.

What has brought you back to the village?

The river is a screen against sins, its waters the tears of the repentant.

Shafak left the bridge in the direction of the river. When she reached the bank her feeling of self-deprecation increased: she had the sensation of floating on a scandal and she remembered her impure act.

She was seized with the longing, before death, to see her grandmother, her mother, and her grandfather the omda, and she moaned without tears. She went out into the turbid light of day toward the river.

A solitary fisherman (not of this village) had spread out his gown on the earth floor of the bridge and had performed the two prescribed prostrations of the morning prayer, with the reed basket alongside him. He at once spreads out his net and hears the clinking of its lead weights. He casts it into the river without any certainty that it will bring him provision for his day or just stones and mud.

The sound of the girl's body striking the water alerts him. Then he throws himself into the river and swims toward the body that rises and sinks in the water.

2

The grandfather: an omda and the son of an omda.

He came from a tree whose roots struck down deeply in time and place. He was of ancient stock, born of strangers from far-off lands who had passed away, riding horses that whinnied in the wastelands, making conquests as they went until they settled in Egypt, that land protected by God.

From a dynasty of peers, having status and power, with obedience and service required of their slaves, he would go out in style from the mansion, grasping his ivory stick and dressed in a blue broadcloth cloak.

He had spent two sleepless nights since the fisherman had rescued his granddaughter from the river.

He stood in front of the door of the official reception room, contemplating the days, counting the years, and thinking with heavy heart of his granddaughter, who, at the end of his life, had struck him a blow right to his entrails and defiled the shawl round his turban.

His tired eyes betrayed his perturbed state and his exhaustion, which his clean clothes could not conceal.

He regarded, inside the reception room, the old desk with sculpted woodwork. On the desk stood the official black telephone with its crooked arm; there was the detention room for criminals with a large padlock on the door; and the armory with its seven rifles locked in place with a heavy metal chain that was tarnished, and with a solitary guard overcome by sleep waiting for his orders.

The omda stared back at him when he felt that he was looking into his eyes deviously.

It was a day with a heavy wind, and an old blind man had lit himself a fire close by and was sitting warming himself by it.

He gave a deep sigh and whispered to himself, "It all ends in ignominy. The girl came out of the river bringing disgrace with her."

The wind stirred the earth of the winter month of Amsheer, raising the soot from the ground. It begrimed his face, the shawl around his turban, and the broadcloth cloak. Would that those who had vanished from sight did not come back, did not bring pain to his heart! There were tarbooshes proudly worn, caftans of striped cotton and silk, hitching places for the horse, and silver candlesticks for giving light to the vast rooms of the mansion and for guest rooms with their many couches.

He spread out his cloak and it filled with wind.

At the top of the street he saw a gathering of people making their way noisily toward the reception room: women and men and young children crying out, while he stood there confused like an animal at bay.

Smarting rays of winter sunshine began to pierce through the lotus-fruit tree on the bridge. The air became filled as if with the smell of the blood of parturition with the crowd approaching the reception room.

"Hurry up, Your Excellency—it's that boy Hasan, the son of Sherifa. They caught him on the roof of the Allawina house." The boy's wrists were bound with twine, and blood was dripping from his nose, while a suppressed scream, a call for help, was voiced by the expression on his face.

The omda motioned with his hand and everyone fell silent. Having sent them away, he locked the boy in the reception room, where he sat close to the wall, dripping blood.

He contemplates him now unhappily, with a heavy conscience and a spirit that is captive. His hand pushes aside the cloak that every now and again slips down from his body. Then he goes back to gazing at the road that slopes down to the river, his mind still not free of the girl's act, as he thinks about the punishment and how to save his sullied honor.

He was looking at the boy's eyes: a certain shadow of disdain peered out from the redness of the flowing blood, while a sly smile flickered on the split lips.

"Even the thieves and the roadside dogs are laughing at you. How can you regain your stature after the whip has been mislaid in the storeroom? Here you are at the end of your life with your head in the dirt!"

He approached the boy with halting steps. With a trembling hand he undid the fetters and wiped the blood from him. Then, with unprecedented sympathy, he pointed in the direction of the road.

He who had never once yielded was struggling, as he stood there, to keep back the tears of an old man.

3

The house slave was in front of the mansion getting the carriage ready. A top of shining leather edged with silver, two large wheels to take it on its journeys, colored in blue and red, the rear seat covered with a piece of old-fashioned velvet in green with a small seat opposite it, while on the floor was spread a sheepskin as clean as spun silk. On each side was a brass lamp like pure gold, with white glass, that hung down and gave out a decorative light like the candles at the celebrations of the seventh day after birth or the lamps of those who have lost their way.

"And when I was young, the son of poor folk, I'd hear the carriage coming from the provincial capital at night, the horse trotting. I would be woken from the depths of sleep and I'd get up and look down on it from the window of the winter room, and I'd glimpse the light from the two lamps piercing the darkness of the night as though some hand in the gloom were pushing them, or they were being carried on the wind, and I didn't see the horse, nor yet the slave Owais, not even the ladies, but only the two lamps as though in a dream."

The horse gleams in the sun and the carriage shines with the thrust of the noon rays as it waits for the lady grandmother to make her appearance, coming down from the mansion and going to the town, followed by her daughters in garments of velvet and natural silk.

A grandmother from of old, a lady whose voice would carry from one end of the village to the other if she gave an angry shout.

"The village is mine, and he who doesn't like it can go find himself some other village."

Wealth that pierced like a blade the hearts of the poor, driving them to walk in the shade of walls: obedience was obligatory and as everlasting as a tattoo on the chest.

Trays of food at the time of funerals. Gifts of money at circumcision ceremonies. Large tents set out at religious festivals. The paying out of money in fulfillment of some old vow.

Generosity supported by riches and the desire to show off.

The grandmother sits in her room, with the curtains in the house drawn, regarding pictures on the wall of high-ranking officials with twirled mustaches, swords and firearms from past times displayed.

She got up with frowning face, her head uncovered and hair disheveled. The winter wind was tossing her hair about.

She stood on the balcony of the house that looked over the village. People had never seen her before with hair disheveled. At that moment it seemed to them that she was some sprite that had emerged from the water.

"It's as though I were searching for a tear for my eye," she said to herself.

Frightened to break down, she braced herself. Then she called out insanely: "I'll wring her neck with my own hands so that no one in the village can say that I've turned a blind eye to her losing her honor . . ."

The wind whistled high above the saint's minaret.

4

The father of the girl was looking abstractedly at the night.

The catastrophe of his daughter went around and around in his mind. He continually remembered her childhood when he would take her behind him on the horse and would gallop with her over the bridge. She would insist that he dismount from the horse so that she could lead it.

He was contemplating the mood of the mansion and had a feeling of contraction in his chest. He was living on the top floor of a house whose windows all looked over the fields, the course of the river, and the saint's tomb.

How was he going to face her without collapsing or cutting her throat?

He got up and went in search of his wife in the many rooms. He opened his father's north-facing room only to find it empty. He realized that his father was now in the general reception room, in flight from what was inevitable.

He branched off to the right and opened the grandmother's room. She was seated on the couch, rendered speechless by the catastrophe, her hair undone. She was not aware of him as he opened the door. The place was joyless, haunted by sudden fears and an overall sense of scandal.

He did not want to face the girl on his own; he wished to have his wife with him. He was frightened of his weakness and his love for the girl, who had come after seven boys, and the world appeared to him to be filled with things that were vile and dirty.

He walked along the corridors of the mansion as though they were underground pathways in a cavern, separated one from the other.

Isolated rooms in mourning, gloomy and old. He no sooner opened a room than he closed it again, finding only bare walls and hanging lamps giving no light. No one.

Demolished as though by death itself and a catastrophe withering his life and those of his ancestors. The two aunts had taken refuge in their rooms, while the servants had hidden themselves from sight. Even with the slave Owais, it was as if he had inhaled the smell of the simoom wind and had melted into thin air. He began hurrying through the house like someone plunging through a pitch-black night.

He reached his wife's room, took hold of the doorknob and turned it. The light blinded him and he lowered his gaze. Collecting himself, he looked ahead of him.

His unchaste daughter was squatting in the bathing basin, her body filling it. Her limbs could be seen under the light as she seemed to float in the foam of scented soap, naked under the lamplight. The mother was holding a brass ewer in her left hand and pouring warm water over her daughter, as though to cleanse her of her defilement.

He heard his wife's whimpering as she massaged the girl's body in repeated circular movements, with the water flowing down into the basin right up to the rim.

The scene looked unreal to him. It seemed to him that he heard the whinnying of a horse coming from the stables, quickly growing louder.

5

"The slave's a slave, and the master's a master: one link attached to another. Keep quiet, Auntie Umm al-Saad—the world has taught me much."

"Brother, all of us are the children of nine months."

"That's just talk, Auntie, while the truth stabs you in the eye."

To his right was the stable for the animals and the male mulberry tree, and to his left the water channel, on both banks of which grew uncultivated trees and in whose depths flitted fish the size of one's hand. "These are my father's words, taken from my grandfather who was sold in the slave market at Imbaba."

"That was a long time ago and times have changed."

"Nothing has changed. Black is black and white is white."

In anger he pushed the wedge of wood into the knot made by the rope and began moving the blade of the plow until it penetrated the dry ground that had been well watered. He cracked the whip and the two animals, held together by the wooden yoke, moved off.

The tooth of the plow bit into the earth, splitting it open and revealing old roots, live worms and broken shells, the remains of ancient bones, shards with mysterious writing on them, and the remnants of roots from past seasons.

The aunt and the young man, who both serve in the large house in return for their keep, walk together. He pushes the plow while she, with bent back, breastless, head held down towards the ground, has slung on her shoulder the reed basket in which are moistened grains of corn that she lets slip through her fingers into the uniform lines, as she chews toothlessly at her cheeks.

Pushing the plow with his foot, his face gleams with sweat. He draws the rope taut to keep the animals to a straight line.

The black youth sighs sadly with the thought that a whole mansion is on his shoulders.

Hedges to be cut, provision bags to be filled, animals to be milked in the morning shift and at night, crops to be gathered.

"What's going on now?" he asks himself.

The young lady's gone and done it, so that's that.

For days on end the mansion was locked up, with my lady Shafak imprisoned and with visitors no longer coming.

In the past he used to see her standing under the pomegranate tree in the garden of the house, her scent blowing onto him, with the smell of the garden roses, and his heart would start, and he would be careful not to do anything wrong, and when she shouted at him he would take to his heels.

"Even the old lady has vanished into thin air."

At night he let himself wander around the mansion, hoping he would come to understand what had happened.

6

The grandfather was chairing the meeting, with the grandmother facing him, and the father and uncles sitting under the window open to the night, not realizing how much time had passed without their saying anything.

The girl was in the center, sitting on the ground, clean and recently bathed, with a smell of perfume about her.

Suddenly the mares neighed, as in the springtime when they wish to be covered. The night grew heavy with their neighings and the father fought against his anger. He rose and leaned out of the window and screamed at Owais the slave, "Shut 'em up, you bastard, or I'll come down and do for you."

The slave, who was sitting squat-legged in front of the stable door, leaped to his feet. The father returned to his place and sat down.

The grandfather straightened his clothes and looked at the faces of his family seated under the faint light of the isolated guest room.

"What's happened has happened by fate, and we're not a family that knows how to kill."

"Let's marry her off, Father," said the aunt in a low voice. "Marriage is a shield and there are thousands who would be pleased to do it for us."

The grandfather lowered his head and regarded the ground at his feet.

The father got up and waved his hands about. "Nobody's going to remove my shame but me."

"Sit down, Fikri, let's talk sensibly."

The father went up to the window and looked out at the night. The grandfather directed his words at the girl. "Happy about it all, Shafak?"

"Do as you see best, Grandpa," she answered dejectedly.

There had been a tenderness in his quavering voice: the flow of blood that joined him to that girl.

The grandmother was silent, fixing them with the eyes of a bird of prey. Suddenly she shouted at them: "That's the talk of weak old women. The omda's heart is too sensitive. I'll not spare her with death."

The night settled down, and all at once the storms of Amsheer abated, then quickly renewed themselves.

The wintry moon was making its hesitant way through the clouds of winter, and a stinging cold kept people's bodies immobilized.

They gazed in fear at the grandmother.

She rose with her upright body that had never been bent. They could hear the beating of their hearts as they waited for her to have her final say.

They knew that she was searching for a punishment.

She strode ahead past them, then turned and looked into their eyes. At the window she gazed out at the night and the things left about. A light showed up the garden wall, the marble steps. The cry of a curlew carried from the river.

She was surveying the place with her gaze until it alighted upon the man sitting under the light of the lamp in front of the stables, his hand still holding a piece of firewood, his color not showing up in the night and nothing being heard except his sighing.

Owais, the man born of slaves, was sitting in the night under a sparse light, waiting as he gazed up at the window of the guest room where the family was gathered.

The grandmother regarded him as though seeing him for the first time. Her eyes roved between him and her granddaughter. Then she gave a sigh of relief, as though restored to health, after which she closed the window.

The Man With the Traps

"And how's it all going to end?"

I heard myself uttering these words as I started up from the depths of sleep, as though it were the sting of inner time that suddenly occurs, accompanying the strokes of the clock hanging on the wall, whose striking rings out throughout the house so that you get up.

I was awake.

"Certain things that relate to you occur around you, and because they are frighteningly evil you imagine that it is the Devil who has contrived them."

I got up feeling the sultriness of noon weather replete with oppressive humidity and the mountain dust. I wiped away the sweat with the palm of my hands and looked out of the bedroom to where the mass of the river lock lies, the construction of which I am supervising. It was crouching there silently like some animal, with the debris excavated from it making a mound of sand on both sides. No one had yet put foot on the site today, which happened to be a holiday.

I regarded the makeshift furnishings of my house. Always I live in temporary lodgings set up near the boundaries of deserts, where irrigation projects begin at the mouths of canals and end inside faraway sands. My desk is beside the window. Books on the shelf and on the floor. Chairs made of palm leaves here and on the balcony overlooking the dirt track edged by eucalyptus trees. A plan of the project site on the wall and a drawing of the lock. A number of earthenware water jugs are cooling on the sill. A pomegranate tree in an ancient garden, dusty and devoid of fruit.

"And how's it all going to end with that son of a crazy woman?"

I passed my hand across my forehead against the feeling of dizziness, grinding my teeth with the fury of someone impotent to thrust evil away from himself. I asked myself: what can I do, I who am stuck out here at the construction site of the lock, to repel what is happening to me? How can I come to know the impulses of others toward me, I who have been worn out by my good feelings toward them, people whose minds conceal grudges against one?

From the very beginning the thing had started like some stupid joke.

A week ago I took the jeep from the lock site to go to the city where the company had its head office. I was sitting behind the driving wheel, pressing down on the accelerator as I tried to escape from my continued preoccupation with this never-ending project. Arriving at the asphalt road, I branched left and put on speed.

I arrived at the souk area in the city. It was crowded with people; fruit and vegetables from the mountain land filled the large covered wholesale markets, with lorries lined up awaiting their turn, and the voices of the bidders at the auctions mingling with the dust of the street, the neighing of horses, and scorching noon heat.

I spotted him standing in ragged khaki clothes in the middle of a knot of people. His leg was amputated at the thigh and he was supporting his weight on a crutch, while around his shoulders were fastened several serrated metal traps. He was opening and closing his mouth excitedly. He seemed to be in a nervous state and was lifting up his crutch and waving it about, and the traps gave out a clanging sound above the heads of the crowd massed around him.

When he saw me, he forced his way through the people in my direction, bounding along on his one leg and waving his crutch in the air. He stood in front of the door of the truck, staring with fixed gaze at me. I looked into his eyes: they were not those of a man in his right senses but those of someone deranged. As he came nearer he gave out a smell of ashes and the sourness of old tobacco. His face was pitted and exuded a greenish-yellow color like that of seaweed.

I saw him raising his crutch as he tried to get it in through the window so as to thrust it against my chest.

"Just you wait!" he shouted. "You'll be meeting your end at my hands yet."

Over the sound of the clanging of his traps, he spoke about his daughter with the jet-black tresses, the magical singing voice, and the sea-blueness of her eyes, the girl who spoke several languages and whom he had lost when she had vanished into the mountain.

"It's him, it's him," he said, pointing at me and directing his words at the crowd.

As their clamor grew louder, I tried to open the door and go down to him, but he had taken his crutch and, putting it under his arm, had begun limping off like some crow until he had disappeared in the jostlings of the souk.

The wind rose up, coming from the mountain and bringing sand with it. I felt dejected. The people were looking in my direction accusingly. I was incapable of understanding what was happening in front of me. It all seemed somehow incomprehensible. So, to escape my feelings of confusion, I drove toward the company offices. Entering by the front door, I went up the stairs to the engineering section. I saw my colleagues lifting their heads to gaze at me, then ignoring me as they looked down at their papers. There was an unnatural atmosphere in the place: a sense of awkwardness encompassed them all.

"Good morning."

The reply was mixed, unclear, hurried: incoherent murmurs, and they busied themselves about their work so as not to look at me.

I drew out a chair and sat down beside the secretary.

"Anything wrong?" I asked him.

"Nothing at all."

"What's wrong with you all?"

He hesitated for a moment, then tapped his pen against the glass top of the desk as he looked at me from under his glasses.

"The fact is . . . "

"What?"

"This man with the amputated leg . . . "

"What about him?" I said.

"He came here and kicked up a fuss and went in to see the manager."

"What about?"

"He was saying all sorts of things: vague unintelligible things. He talked about you and some daughter of his. What's it all about?"

"All about?—I've never seen the fellow in my whole life. What's his job?"

"He says he's a hunter."

He was silent for a moment, then looked toward me and said, "Why has he got it in for you like this? Even as he left his office, we saw the manager patting him on the shoulder and we heard him saying to him at the door, 'Don't worry, everything will be fine and you'll get your rights.'"

The secretary went back to his work and it seemed to me that what was happening now was even more obscure and frightening.

I felt that someone was secretly concocting something against me, something that was making me hate my life.

I thought about the man with the amputated leg hopping along on his crutch and carrying his traps on his shoulder. I tried, sitting there, to concentrate my mind and search about in my memory for him.

Perhaps, somewhere, I had met him by chance or had seen him in some dream, but I was unable to find any connection to him.

Without another word, I rose to my feet and left the company's offices.

The jeep hurtled toward the mountain. It looked desolate, devoid of any friendly intimacy. The little greenness that tattooed the face of the earth had gone; seas of sand followed one after the other, and sudden gusts of wind whirled around the dry grasses. Avoiding the steep slope, the truck gave its back to the turbid emptiness and took to the canal road.

Later on, I saw him, aloof in the morning mist, almost unseen in the haze and the reed canes, pointing in my direction with his crutch, then quickly disappearing from view.

I wished I could come to some understanding with him and ask him what he wanted, but he would hurriedly disappear after inciting people against me, pronouncing my name, and talking about his daughter who had disappeared in the mountain, the girl with the nocturnal locks, a magic voice, and with the sea looking out from her eyes, the girl who could speak several languages.

Two days ago I was at the work site. The frame of the lock was being pressed into the mountain; in the center was an iron lock gate, at the top of which were two cogwheels for opening it. The workmen were coming up out of the earthwork like ants, while a vast dinosaur thrust its outstretched hand into the sand, casting it up onto the mountain.

He was standing right there, right at the top, with his ragged mustache and ash-smelling khaki clothes, a vague smile on his greenish face. He was supporting his shoulder on the crutch, which was thrust into the sand; his trouser-leg, empty of flesh and bone, flapped about in the wind.

I clambered up the sand using both hands, trying to reach the man whose long disheveled hair was being tossed about in the wind. I saw him backing away and going down behind the dunes as I stood at the mountain peak, gazing down at an emptiness where there was not a living soul.

A thread of smoke; a dwelling under a trellis inhabited by stray cats; a sun emerging from the gown of night every daybreak. I seem to be like someone astray, in whose veins fall drops of strong acid.

The man with one leg, the traps hanging round him, and all those people I know and for whom I have a special affection.

"The man playing this stupid joke," I tell myself, "will soon tire of it."

What's this that's happening to me? In this place far from any inhabited area, between the jostling city and the isolated mountain?

Tired, I rose from my bed. The night was about to come.

I made myself tea and wrung out the clothes I had washed. I went up to the balcony to hang them on the line. I looked out and found him by the wooden trellis beside the water pump. When he saw me on the balcony, he rattled the traps, then swore at me and cursed my thieving bastards of forebears. Then, hobbling off, he disappeared in the field of cactus.

The traps hanging round his shoulders puzzled me. I realized they were there for some crime, and I resolved to go to the company in the morning and to ask for a guard.

I found him near the fence to the house. He had put his crutch to one side and seemed to be engaged in setting something up around the fence. I recoiled in fear. I felt he had approached too close, that he was trying in some way to reach right into my house.

"Stay where you are! What are you up to?" I shouted.

He raised his head and looked in my direction.

I don't know how much time passed as I stared into the night. All I know is that it came suddenly: a strangled cry that turned into a howling scream, sharp and continuous, a scream that pleaded help from the very mountain itself.

I put my feet in my slippers and took up the lamp. I descended the stairs, making my way in the direction of the screaming. My shadow was behind me and followed me. It was as though I were moving in a dream, a nightmare.

By the outside gateway I saw him in the light from the lamp. One of the traps he had set had closed over him and he lay in a pool of blood. He stretched out a hand toward me as though seeking help.

"So, it's you," I said. Having made sure who it was, I returned to the house and closed the door behind me.

The Tracker

For several years now, pleasures have been few and far between in these parts.

My confused memory is no longer aware of having laughed from the heart throughout those years. No sooner had the star of the pederast and the butcher, of the man of property and the nightclub dancer, the biographer, the mendacious historian, and the banker risen high in the sky of the happy homeland than I became convinced that things had changed. I told myself, "Watch out—you must look around for that which is unfamiliar."

In any event—and despite this permanent sadness—I set about pursuing a strange hobby, a hobby that provoked both laughter and astonishment: it consisted of daubing dates on pieces of old wood. In order to feel passionately for such wood, you had to sacrifice the time you were in and to open your heart to a dialogue with the years.

I used to hang around in disguise until there was no one about and only a few lamps were alight in front of the houses. Then I would stealthily emerge from my place of hiding, climb up walls and rip out pieces of wood from the façades I had previously earmarked and take them back to where I lived. Thus, directly I opened the door of my apartment and entered, there would come to me the odor of a time that had been made captive, all mixed up with the smell of those living things I had collected that do not become obsolete.

I used to drag out a bench, so old it was pitiful, with short legs decorated with seven-pointed stars encircled by flowers connected to outstretched branches. I would put on an ancient gramophone the cracked record of that melancholy Turkish singing interspersed with *"Aman! Aman!"* that brings one to the verge of tears. I would remain meditating on the voice and asking myself about the meaning of fulfilled yearnings and about those suns that have risen and passed on.

The ancient clock strikes the hour of one in the emptiness of the sitting room. I look toward it, not knowing whether it has been put right or whether there is a mingling of times. I spend my night immersed in a delirium that numbs my body as I try to escape from the feeling, fearful of the terror that quickly descends upon my heart after this state of delirium withdraws. The morning comes upon me and I hear the sound of the departing train, see clouds in the sky and prepare myself for sleep, indulging in the hope of dreaming some old dream.

At night I climb the mountain and see the old quarter dozing in its embrace, and I go down into alleyways that lead to other alleyways, and no sooner have I started to walk in them than I see the sultan's mosque, alongside which beggars sleep, glimpsing from afar the shadow of the guards standing under the lamps.

As I was proceeding slowly in my wandering, involuntarily advancing further and further, I was met by a seeker after learning, a hurrying woman, someone reading fortunes, and the chief of the night patrol.

I was filled with the smell of incense as I walked in the fields of ginger whose tracks were tattooed with colored pebbles.

Ever since I had known that nothing but the Face of God endures, I have also been convinced that nothing is lost, especially in this night that has attained its final third when He prepares Himself to pass from the darkness to the light, while I am standing before one of His old doors near the lamp that illuminates for me what I shall be tearing away. I looked—with true love—across the lane and called out, seeking His protection.

When I had scaled the outer wall and was wrenching from the latticework the wooden star, the nail became jammed and gave out a piercing sound. I don't know why a woman should have put her head out of the window and screamed "Thief!"—and I was astonished at the speed with which people gathered.

I was looking down at them, suspended as I was between God's house in the sky and the earth that had brought forth all those creatures, and I heard them shouting at me, "Come down, thief!" I descended, crawling down the wall and scraping myself against the protuberances that mercilessly pressed into my chest, I who loved them during all my days.

No sooner had I made it to the ground than someone gave me a kick in the groin, so that I went automatically into a crouching position and clutched at myself, saying "Oh!" Another gave me a kick in the face with his bare foot and I heard the sound of breaking bones. My heart cried out with the pain and circles of variegated colors flashed out, after which blows from trained arms rained down on me. I don't know why it was that, as they were beating me, I recollected my dead mother and had the impression that I heard her voice.

They conducted me along the alleyway surrounded by their sneers and scoffing. Their voices came to me with a whistling in my ears, and I heard a man talking about the police and the nearby police station. When I asked him why they were beating me, they looked at me with hatred and shouted in my face: "Get a move on, thief!" I saw them turning off in the direction of the alleyway clothed in shadows, coming out into the spacious square, and I saw a door being opened and a white-haired old man peering out, wearing a caftan of striped material and standing leaning against the door. When he asked them, "What's up with him?" they answered, "A thief." He shook his head and smiled and I heard him mutter "Thief? What's there left to steal? There's nothing left—they've taken everything." I found him going back to a low, round, wooden table, on top of which rested an iron with a long handle, the kind whose time had long passed. As I moved away I could hear the banging of the iron and its echo in the night.

In the square was a disused tramline, and a mausoleum to the Lady Zaynab, the Prophet's granddaughter. On the platform, villagers were sleeping, resting against their provisions for the journey stuffed inside baskets made of palm fronds and reeds.

The police station was an old building put up by a khedive who had died and been buried in the cemetery of the Imam Shafi'i. I was attracted by the picture of the departing angel, the wall painting, and the symmetrical *Naskh* calligraphy. I was not at ease, and each time I looked at the thread of blood flowing down from my nose, I lost my confidence. I said to the man gripping my hand, "Look—the angel." He shouted at me, "Shut up, you thief."

We went up the eight steps to the police station. Under the lamp at the entrance I saw the blood on my chest and my pitiful torn shirt.

They told the officer my story and he gave me a slap on the face and questioned me with shouts about my name, my address, and my occupation. Another person answered him. "He's a thief, sir." When I remained silent he gave me another slap and said, "Answer, you son of a dog."

I wiped my clouded-up glasses and contemplated his face, which reminded me of the faces of the pigs at the place they are kept in the Mokattam Hills. I smiled and looked into his face. He slapped me, shouting, "Have you no shame!" I said to him that nothing is lost and that what appears dead to him is alive to a frightening degree. When in astonishment he shook his head uncomprehendingly, I talked to him about peacocks and Persian fire and the letters in *Naskh* calligraphy and the scent of captive time.

When I had finished, he sucked at his lip and I heard him murmur, "It's sad," and he placed his hand on my shoulder and dismissed the people, who did not understand.

The officer sat me down in front of his desk, ordered me tea, and wiped the blood from my face. Then he dismissed me with a warning, and no sooner had I reached the door than I heard his colleague ask him, "Where's he going?" To which he replied shortly, "To the sanitarium—the Devil take him! He's gone crazy."

I went out into the street, where daylight was about to appear. When I looked eastward, I murmured, "Maybe it's going to rain soon."

After the incident at the police station, I replaced climbing up walls with passing by antique shops.

Huda Sharawi Street was my preferred area. Its houses were all of one style, also its Fatimid mosque with the spacious courtyard and enormous dome facing the towers of the Ukhuwwa Church, whose bells ring out with that weighty sound.

I used to stand in front of the shop windows enraptured by what I saw. I calculated the number of shops and knew the most important items they contained. I attributed to each item its date and style.

I made friends with the owners and would sit with them, and they would allow me to photograph as I wanted, and I kept the pictures in my apartment together with the pieces of wood, the cracked records, and those old books with yellowish pages.

When the antique shops were converted into a bank, a restaurant, a garage, automobile showrooms, and a travel agency, the last of the traders advised me to go off to the auctions. Despite my chronic poverty, I made a point of attending such auctions, after learning of the salons in which they were held and the quarters in which those salons were to be found. I followed the sale dates with uninterrupted frenzy, filling my wallet with advertisements from the papers containing details of what was being put up for sale.

My destination today was a villa in Garden City, which I had read about in yesterday's *al-Ahram* paper. I saw the Nile, contemplated its greenish water and said to myself, "It's been stored for too long." As I drew close to the villa, my mind unfolded and my heart filled with the elation of walking in the open air. Because of my fear that I might lose my elation, I recited some verses of poetry and watched the young girls walking along the bank in colored clothes and ribbons. I said to them, "Going to the auction?" and they burst out laughing at my strange, disordered appearance.

I met the theology teacher at the bend of the street. I saw him standing under a tree with a large-sized book under his arm and gazing at the other bank of the river. He was wearing his black monastic garb and on his chest there dangled a wooden cross, while in his other hand was a rosary of yellow amber. As I approached closer, his features became clearer and a contented smile showed on his lips. I was standing in front of him when he said, "Where to?" and I said to him, "To the auction, Father." He smiled at my calling him 'Father.'

He took me by the hand and a deathly coolness penetrated me. "He's grown old," I told myself. "Did you say anything?" he asked with a smile. I shook my head in denial. I looked into his eyes. My mind wandered among the monks' cells and was captivated by the galaxies, and I saw thin, emaciated bodies waiting doggedly in the midst of immemorial chants. I felt as if the Day of Judgment would come while I was walking on ground that had not been touched by fire, looking at the city from that magnificent height.

"How you have aged, Father!" I said to him, and he bent over my ear and said, "It's the years of living in the monastery."

He astonished me when he opened his waistcoat and revealed his chest, where I saw a tattoo of a ravishingly beautiful woman. I said to him, "I don't understand," and he answered me, "One must persevere," so I talked to him about the impossible, about knocking on closed doors, and the tears of the accursed, and I explained to him about my disease for which there is no cure.

I left him buttoning up his waistcoat and looking in the direction of the river. It seemed to me that I heard him making a sound as of weeping.

The time had come for me to collect myself and hasten on, for the appointed time had drawn close.

A villa with a gate of black iron worked into pointed spearheads. In the middle was a wall of sculpted stone decorated with colors and embellished with jasmine whose scent was diffused through the night and across the paved walkway, on which were outlined black and coffee-colored circles and stars of shining mosaic. Trees heavy with oranges that had not yet ripened. Under a tree in the garden stood a statue in pink marble of a slender, singing slave girl playing a lyre. Hanging around her neck was a piece of paper indicating that she was for sale. Two silver palm trees, from which hung some dates that gave out light, were placed on the first step of the auction salon.

I heard someone playing on the Oriental zither and the pure sound of piano keys being struck.

I read on the outside of the door "Look before the beginnings make their appearance."

I studied it all carefully, placing my hand on my trembling heart, and fingered the few piasters in my pocket. I went up two stairs and read, "Were I to reveal the characteristic of Paradise, I would take you away by illumination from the characteristic."

Am I living the days that have passed? Am I swimming in the times of pearls? (My aim is to take possession of a time that is being lost.) Will my heart continue to be occupied with what has gone before—a prisoner of my constant misgivings?

Entering by the door, I was astonished at what met my eyes: a medley of human beings in conventional clothing. The men wore black evening dress, while the women showed themselves off in décolleté gowns on which, in the glaring light of the hall, sparkled pieces of jewelry.

When I entered they all stared at me, then grew silent, though they quickly continued talking.

It was as if I knew them, had seen them previously, those faces with common features and identical mysterious smiles. All these expressions I had met before—perhaps in paintings or in some ceremony in commemoration of someone deceased.

I saw them smiling slyly and pointing toward me. I ignored them and concerned myself with the tableaux on the walls and the bibelots on the shelves. There were also porcelain vases, paintings in old frames from past epochs, candelabra and items of old furniture stacked up by the walls, and oil lamps that had lit up palaces through the passing of the years, now bestowing light as though part of some ancient funeral cortège.

The auctioneer climbed up to his place and struck a table with his hammer. He began opening the auction by speaking into a small microphone.

"Two Sèvres vases from the time of Napoleon, depicting a lady holding in her hand a golden ear of wheat, with branches of silver. Who will bid me a thousand?"

"A thousand one hundred."

"A thousand five hundred."

"Two thousand—each vase a thousand."

"Two thousand," echoed the auctioneer's voice. "Who'll bid me more? Two thousand. How cheap! One, two, three."

Silence descended as the two vases went to the final bidder. A set of French Louis Quinze Aubusson chairs, depicting people of the time, and with them a Louis Seize table inlaid with silver from the same period.

"Who'll bid four thousand?"

"Four thousand five hundred."

"Five thousand."

"Six."

"Six thousand," repeated the auctioneer. "Six thousand. Cheap at the price. Congratulations."

The works of art were shown one after the other in the light. Epochs of time mingled with one another.

Chinese carpets and others from Kashan and Isfahan. A round Tabriz carpet with a border in gold thread and the picture of a peacock spreading its tail near a fountain of colored water. Two Venetian black slaves with sparkling eyes. A Japanese drawing of the trunk of a tree with seed pearls and flowers with imperial crowns. An old drawing in pastel by an unknown artist of a fortress by the sea facing a sailing ship plowing its way through high waves. A candelabrum and chandelier of Turkish style that had illuminated the halls of sultans and in whose light dancing slave girls had swayed. A mirror in a frame of arabesque rosewood inlaid with ivory and shells from the China Seas. A Chinese statue of the Buddha sitting in traditional pose and smiling. A picture, one meter by one meter, painted by an artist who had lived in Alexandria in the middle of the last century.

"Two thousand. Cheap at the price. The frame alone is worth it. Look at the coloring and the patina."

A picture of a Sufi wearing a waistcoat of broadcloth with fiery bright eyes that stared out of a tired face. A picture in black and white of the Aqsa Mosque with a bird resembling an eagle flying above it, wings outstretched, its shadow falling on the dome.

The auctioneer moved the microphone away from his mouth and fell silent.

The people looked at him, also in silence.

"The surprise of the auction: a legacy of grandparents to their grandsons."

He lifted up a box and took from it a pendant lamp with a silver chain that ended in a hook. On its left side were rubies, while on the right was a line of writing inlaid with three different precious stones, glittering like stars. I read the first line: "Make known to me the knowledge of certainty."

My heart beat and my breath became imprisoned within me as cold sweat broke out on my forehead. I felt as though reaching the borders of a dream— my loneliness amid living ruins coming to an end, and at last recognizing that nothing is lost, nothing is gone.

"A pendant lamp. It illuminated nights of yore, the palaces of kings, the bedchambers of harems, the tents of knights, the khans of copyists. Who'll bid me ten thousand?"

The bidding had started high and the bidders were taken aback. The silence of surprise enveloped them. I heard the zither playing an Oriental melody. I lay back on cushions of silk as I looked at the lamp that gave light without oil.

I felt in my pocket and cursed my ill luck. Then, taking control of myself, my voice called out, somewhat hesitantly, "I bid twelve thousand."

A murmuring of voices rose up. A man with graying temples and a chain that ended in a blue medallion came into view. He smiled at me and said, "I bid fifteen thousand."

Another said, "I bid seventeen thousand."

A woman in décolleté called out, "Exorbitant!"

"The piece is worth it."

"I bid twenty thousand," I called out in a confident tone. When the bidding ended with your humble servant, I heard a woman whisper to another, "He's the middleman for someone rich."

The auctioneer demanded an advance. I asked him to wait while I wrote out a check. I sat myself in an armchair in the corner and bided my time.

At the end of the evening the auction came to a close and I found myself alone with the owner, the auctioneer, and the men guarding the place.

When the auctioneer said to me, "Where's the check?" I said, "What check?" His eyes widened in astonishment and he replied angrily, "The check for the pendant lamp." He looked toward the owner and whispered in his ear, "A con man." The man answered him, "Or a madman." He was silent, then he said, "He has cost us a deal. Shut him up in the storeroom and tomorrow hand him over to the police."

When I found myself imprisoned in the semi-darkness and had seated myself among the creations of God in a state of inner harmony, though burning with exhaustion, I said to myself, "No time is further away than any other. Destiny has incarnations in destiny." I asked myself about the extent of my commitment to these things that had been piled up, and I heard the voice of the muezzin while I had still not yet dozed off. I was sitting on a carpet, and the Lord was granting me some of His pride, while I heard the playing of the zither with the Maghribi melody and saw the porcelain dancer come out from among the other works of art and perform to the rhythm of the zither. I stared up at the ceiling and saw the pendant lamp all lit up, traversing the rooms in luminous circuits, giving light without oil, thus intensifying the melody and revealing a thin man treading on a surface of sand and looking toward where the setting suns glimmered. It was as if he were a Sindbad made of colored plaster of Paris, whose ship had sailed away to the distant lands of Java, leaving behind, after a voracious experience, seashores of wonder, planted with sarcenet and saffron. That journey of his which he had recounted had aroused the disapproval of a handful of impostors, people of poor imagination who appeared to his eye to be permanent objects of ridicule, for they were incapable of understanding him. He is one of the last scions of those men of insight who live on dreams. He made them understand that the world is not one, and that despite being round it is many worlds, and that beginnings possess, eventually, endings, and that he—Sindbad—was capable of boarding ships and embarking boldly upon seas, and of staring into suns, even if they are setting, in order to see at a distance the Persian cities and Mameluke domes, and to hear such names as Bokhara and Samarqand. Thus he appeared to himself and to others, because of the long time he had adored the orchestra of essence, in order to become one of the time-honored trackers.

The Gazelle Hunter

Leaning on the banisters, she goes down the stairs until she reaches the front door. Opening it, she remains quietly beside the fence, looking out at our aged neighbor as he settles down in his place, as he does every evening, to await the gazelles.

He gazes out at the open space that ends at the mountain, his hand placed on the shoulder of his granddaughter, who leads him about when he gets to his feet.

"Every evening he gets up to see the gazelles," she had said to me.

During that night she died of chronic asthma.

I had heard her whispering to me, "A good funeral, and complete your favor by planting a cactus with four branches, and set up a tombstone with a beautiful front, and be careful to make sure that none of my women neighbors sees me when I'm being washed, and see to it that no blind sheikh recites the Koran over my grave."

I smoothed over the opening to the grave and scoured it with straw and mud.

"From dust to dust," I said.

Having sprinkled some water, I planted a cactus with four branches.

"I'm all alone now, an orphan in old age."

I recalled what she had said to me, a pallid smile on her face: "I wanted to see you as a husband and with children before I died."

However, she died and all she left me was our old house, my inability to deal with people and my avoidance of them, my amazing knowledge of the rising and falling of the stars of destiny and the train timetables, the habit of taking delight in looking at old domes and dreaming of ivory statuettes, and the love of ancient buildings inhabited by worthy ancestors.

And when I had opened the door of her room I was met by the smell of those who have become senile. I asked her to pray for me, while she asked me to make her some cupping glasses because they would show her the faraway shores of Paradise. I brought the glasses, which are shaped like mosque lamps and which, from being so long unused, no longer retain the same old translucence. I began to insert into each glass a screw of burning paper and I affixed them to her back. When I had finished, her back looked to me to be lighted up with unflickering wicks and I could hear her saying to me that she was seeing Paradise.

I was standing by the fence surrounding our dwelling, waiting for my absent father, who would certainly be returning, having hunted some animal. He would be bringing it home on his back and would inquire of me whether she was still seeing the faraway shores of Paradise.

I pulled the cupping glasses off her back and heard them make a sucking noise as the air was released. I saw the wicks that had gone out and changed into black, crumbly ash, settling into the corners of the room, and I saw, in the sparse light of the lamp whose oil had all but run out, that she had dozed off.

I gazed at the pictures hanging on the wall and I realized that after this life of mine I would be the last of the branches of my family and that I was the last to mourn those of them who had departed and to say a few prayers for their souls, and the last to turn out their lamps that give light to the rooms in which feasts had been held.

I realized that I would not find at my death anyone to close my eyelids.

I sucked at my lips and stayed on looking through the window at the desert and listening to the sound of the wind, and I remembered the terror of the gravedigger who heard the same sound roaring inside the cemetery as he was burying her and who raised his head anxiously and called out to me, "There's a roaring noise in the grave," and when I told him it was the wind he went back to completing his job of work.

Our old neighbor who each day sits by the fence had not yet put in an appearance.

However, she had come out of the evening twilight holding in her hand my amulet in a case of sheepskin and sewn with the thread from the intestines of the mountain animals my father had of old been keeping an eye on and which I, when young, would chase right up to where the snakes had their holes. Looking in my direction and raising my amulet to the sun, she had said to me, "You used to wear it until you reached puberty."

I remembered that when I asked her about what the words of the amulet meant, she answered that they were words that preserve life, then she walked off for a while and looked back toward me and said, "In any event, one lives better than all the dead."

Whenever I was overwhelmed by my loneliness I would look at the walls of the house and would be horrified by the thought that I had spent forty years between them, and a feeling of gloom would take hold of me during all this protracted life, causing me many a time to have a sensation of frustration that made me doubt all the circumstances of those old aspirations, aspirations that I used to attribute in past days to some special importance that time had done away with. "In what state," I asked myself, " will I find myself?"

The old man sits by the fence under the trellis of hyacinth bean, with his back resting against the casuarina that makes a sound whenever the wind blows against it, now bearing with it the smell of sands. He looks with small eyes across the extensive plain separating the house from the mountain.

When shade had covered half of the jamb of the window, I used to hear singing coming from the old record, the surface of which glimmered with a patch of blueness, and I saw her wearing the green silk dress figured with wild flowers; it fell loosely over her emaciated frame, a frame which I thought would never be vanquished. When I entered her room, I heard her harsh coughing and realized that

her time was near, and I brought to mind my
grandparents, who had stayed here for a time and
had then departed.

I said to the old man, "You're late," and he
smiled with dimmed gaze and began chewing at his
cheeks with a toothless jaw. "What's the hurry?" he
said to me. "Repetition and the sensation that life is
short protect one from sudden death," I said to
him. "Being distant from an inhabited area is
companionship for loneliness. The place here is cut
off to a terrifying extent." He said to me,
"Loneliness is better than the companionship of evil
people, especially as you know that I have an
appointment with the gazelles." He looked across at
the mountain and went on to say to me, "If one
must die, then at my age I am more worthy of that.
You do not know the truth about the cruelty of life.
You're young and inexperienced to a regrettable
degree. Know that I have not loved anything in life
as I have gazelles. That gentle, affectionate creature.
Have you ever looked into the eye of a gazelle? I
don't think you have." I said to him, "The eye of a
gazelle?" "Yes," he said. Then he said, "I came to
love them after I'd slaughtered so many of them."

He went back to looking at the mountain and to
coughing, when his small body would tremble,
while he would tap the ground with his stick, on
whose crook he would rest his head. "The old man
in front of you," he said to me, "used to be a
professional hunter of gazelles at the time I worked
in Sudan. I spent half my life at it. We used to take
the Land Rover and go off hunting. I would hear

the Sudanese shouting with joy, 'Let's go off hunting as a cure for our spirits.' The desert spaces were open in front of us. We'd be frightened of wild beasts that lived in the forest, expecting them to appear at any moment."

He cleared his throat, coughed and tapped on the ground with his stick. I spotted, hung on his door, a stuffed hawk with outspread wings, which turned with the wind. He went on to say, "The car would chase the gazelles like fate. We wouldn't shoot at them. We would tell ourselves that they'd drop from exhaustion. They would go on galloping to the very end, when I'd look into their eyes, which appealed for release. When they dropped we'd open their bellies while they were still alive and we'd tear out their livers that were boiling from the chase, then we'd cut them into slices, add seasoning, and devour them."

"Alive?" I queried. "Yes, alive," he said to me. "How many such livers I've swallowed!" Then he went on to say, "God will have a day on which He'll call out, 'Arise,' and the bones will gather together above the earth and will rise up." I gave a deep sigh and the memory of the departed swept over me, and I said to him, "No one will rise up and God will not say to the dust 'Rise up.'"

His young granddaughter came out of the house and played under the trellis, then she chased a butterfly and shouted at him, "Grandpa, the sun's going down," and she pointed in the direction of the sun, which pierced its dwelling place in the western reaches.

The old man stood up and put his feet into an old pair of shoes, at which I noticed that his toenails were full of dirt.

The man's shadow trampled over mine and I made way for him. The granddaughter smiled at me with her almond eyes and I passed my hand over her long black hair.

The old man said to me, "I'm leaving." I said to him, "We haven't yet finished our conversation." He answered, "Tomorrow—if it comes—we'll finish it." He turned back to look at the sun near the Lord's house, near His throne, and he said to me, "Don't you see where the sun's got to?"

The girl drew him away from me, and they stirred up the dust as they walked toward the mountain. They began going up to the top, which was not all that high and which was blazing with a twilight like gazelle's blood.

After a while the young gazelles came out from below the mountain. They were leaping about and running toward the old man and his granddaughter. I don't know where they were coming from, but I found the whole mountain filled with their lovely bleating sounds. They were licking the palm of the man's hand in trusting affection. I could hear his voice as if he was sobbing, as the girl passed her hand over his back.

With exhausted spirit, I returned to my home at the borders—having left my soul on the mountain. I walked along the pathway between the yellow flowers and between those who were crossing over to the past where lies God's Fire and His Paradise.

I was surprised to find the living room shining with a light that lit up every corner, the sound of the record loud with Andalusian songs. I placed my hand on my heart and said, "Blessed be the departed," and I inhaled the ancient singing and the odor of the departed, while within me rang out the voice of the old man saying, "Let's go off hunting as a cure for our spirits."

From the top floor her voice came to me, that same voice that called me forty years ago, "Abu Saad, have you come back?"

Like an obedient son I answered, "Yes, Mother, I've come back. I'll lock the door to the passage."

The Blind Sheikh

The call to prayer reverberates.

My cousin surprises me with the words, "The time for prayer has come."

We were walking along the embankment. The village houses were facing us, etching their shadows on the lanes at midday. The streets looked empty and the summer sun was painfully hot. The sound of the call to prayer was one of mercy and solace to the village; it spread in space and struck at my heart with the attachment of times past.

"Who's that?"

"Who?"

"The muezzin."

"Oh, that's Sheikh Bakr al-Ragabi. Have you forgotten him?"

My cousin's face had the color of earth, his eyes a mysterious clarity; he was pitifully thin. We were the same age to the very day and he had a longstanding affection for me despite our lives having taken different paths.

"Do you remember?" my cousin asked.

"Yes."

"The days of Sheikh Bakr, ages ago. It seems you've forgotten."

"The blind man."

"He used to bathe with us in the river. He'd cling onto the steps of the prayer place and would grope about blindly. Do you remember when his hand slipped on the step and he went in, and he continued to go under and come up again, with his screams reaching the ends of the village, and it was you who dragged him out onto dry land?"

"Yes, I remember. All his life he liked me better than the other children. What's he doing now?"

"He performs religious ceremonies, gives the Friday sermon when the imam's away, and goes around as usual in the village, lane by lane and alley by alley."

"He'd been doing it for a long time."

"That's right."

"Thirty years."

"Maybe more."

We crossed the wooden bridge and entered the mosque street, escorted by the inevitable salutations and greetings for the local boy of old.

The mosque had been built in the spacious open square. It was surrounded by eucalyptus and mastic trees, with around it a wall of white brick, which we would often sit astride as if on a horse. We would climb up to it by hanging on to the branches of the mulberry tree that was still standing in the corner on the north side of the mosque. There was a row of latrines and open water taps for making one's ablutions, and coughs commingled with age-old invocations redolent of yearnings for the Divine.

It was the mosque of Abu Hussein in which I had run about and whose minaret I had climbed to complete the call to prayers, and on whose mats I had slept in the blackness of night, a companion for the bats.

I now sat down in the rank of men praying, in front of me the wooden clock that had come to a stop at some time in the past. I saw him rise to his feet with his white gallabiya newly ironed and his four-cornered cap. He raised his broad forehead in the light as he faced the men at prayer. It was Sheikh Bakr, unchanged, with his short body, brown childish face devoid of hair, and his eyes that are lusterless against the darkness. Before ascending the pulpit he called out to the men in a stentorian voice, "Pronounce the Oneness of God."

Throughout the mosque echoed the words, "There is no god but God." He grasped the wooden sword, opened the door of the pulpit and went through it and up the steps.

Sitting there, I could hear the thuds of the sword and the footsteps of the sheikh pushing me back into the past: to the wooden bridge, the river, the school courtyard, our sheikh's Koranic school, my grandfather's ancient loggia and hall where he entertained, and to Sheikh Bakr walking as a boy in the lanes, placing the palm of his hand in front of his eyes and sometimes raising his forehead toward the sun, sometimes toward the stars. He would pass through doors, one door after another. This is the door of Abu Tahoun, this the threshold of the mosque, this the pathway to the cemetery, this the house of Husna—and his voice would soften in tenderness like a gentle breeze.

We would block his way and give him the palms of our hands. We would not speak and he would hold them and run his hand over them for some moments, then face silently into the emptiness around him and surprise you with the words, "Welcome to you," and then say your name. Never once did he make a mistake about the palm of anyone's hand. My own palm would take him mere moments before he recognized it and I would see him tremble as he pronounced my name, "Welcome to you, Abdul Aziz."

I would draw him by the arm and we would go around together until we were standing on the embankment of the river, when I would read to him Nawawi's *Forty Hadiths*, *The Miracles of the Saints*, and the stories of *A Thousand and One Nights*. Then I would recite to him some of the love poems I had written and he would clap his hands with enthusiastic delight at my words. "May the Lord inspire you, Abdul Aziz."

I became conscious of his stentorian voice coming to me from up in the pulpit calling out to the people: "And Abu Ya'qoub al-Sus said: I washed the body of a Sufi novice who had died and he grasped hold of my thumb as he lay on the washing board, and I said: O my son, let go of my hand. I know that you are not dead and that it is merely a migration from one house to another, so let go of my hand."

I was captivated for a moment and my dates and times became all mixed up. It now pained me, the mixing of time and my falling prisoner to what cannot be seen but nonetheless appears to be terrifyingly fundamental.

The men had finished their prayers and were leaving the mosque, having put on their shoes. I was standing just outside, under the branches of the old mulberry tree, looking across the wall to Nawwar Lane and bringing back to mind the story of the girl I had once loved when I was young and who had been drowned.

"Be careful not to open your mouth," I said to my cousin.

I saw the sheikh coming along on his own. He was raising his gallabiya off the ground and holding his shoes in his left hand. As he came closer, I tried to recall his features as they used to be but could only bring to mind his dead, lusterless eyes, the brown complexion, and the four-cornered cap.

I put my hand into his and uttered not a word.

At first his hand ran over mine lightly but soon the movement changed to a quick mechanical one. He pressed down on my hand with both of his as though in search of something forgotten, lineaments that had vanished from his memory as he advanced across age-old obstacles.

What was it that he was trying to arrive at, to call up, that blind old sheikh?

The movement of his hand slowed down and his eyes were upturned, showing a cloudy whiteness. He began breathing heavily as though in pursuit of something unknown.

I felt sorry for him as he tried to conjure up a faraway time, to recall what was almost thirty years, or more, past, the features changed or effaced by the natural action of things.

What are you calling up, O goodhearted blind man?

I was frightened for him in the grip of a crazed rage, so I called out to him, "It wouldn't be reasonable, Sheikh Bakr. After all, it's thirty years."

"I swear by God," he cried in dismay, as though he were on my tail, "if you'd been patient for just a minute longer I'd have known you, Abdul Aziz."

And I took the blind sheikh into my arms.

Modern Arabic Writing
from The American University in Cairo Press